ANTICIPATING REJECTION

SILVIA VIOLET

Anticipating Rejection by Silvia Violet

Cover Art by Amai Designs.

Published in the United States of America.

ONE

Noah pulled a sheet pan of brownies from the oven and set them aside to cool. He'd just started mixing up the mocha icing to top them with when the bakery's front door jangled.

After wiping his hands on a towel, he stepped through the swinging door that separated the kitchen from the sales counter and dining area.

"Good morning, Noah." Ada Crane was far from his favorite person, but she was a frequent customer, and he'd promised his mother he'd be friendly.

He forced a smile. "Good morning, Mrs. Crane. What can I do for you?"

"I need to order a cake. For Saturday."

"Of course; what's the occasion?"

"Haven't you heard? Delford's moving back home."

Noah dropped the notebook of cake ideas. The rings popped open and laminated pages scattered everywhere. "Um… I…"

"Here, let me help you." Noah's mother, Lisa, had been

having coffee with a friend, but she scooted behind the counter and began picking up cake photos.

"Del gets in today, doesn't he?" his mother asked as Noah tried to put the book in order.

"Yes, he does, or at least I hope so. With this blizzard on the way, I can't be sure."

Noah felt like a blizzard was already raging, but it was all inside his head. Del was moving back home? And no one, including his own mother, had bothered to tell him. Why would Del do that? The last Noah had heard, Del had turned his wizard-level math skills into a cushy financial sector job in Chicago.

"When does his flight land?" Noah's mother asked.

"He gets into Casper at six tonight."

His mother nodded. "I don't think the storm is supposed to get bad before then. He should be able to make it."

"Oh, Lisa, I hope so. Edward still can't drive after hurting his leg, so I was going to send Harvey to pick Del up, but some fool cows managed to push down a section of fence, and he's working to fix it before the storm hits. Besides that, he says we've got several cows that could give birth any minute. I told him I'd go, but I do hate driving in bad weather, especially in the dark."

"Oh, you shouldn't make that drive alone with a storm on the way. Noah could go."

"What?" Noah moved his mouth, but no more words came out, mostly because there was nothing he wanted to say to his mother that wasn't profane.

"I can handle the end-of-the-day customers and closing up," his mother said. "There's no reason why you can't get Del at the airport."

She sounded so calm and innocent as she sent him toward his doom. "Mom, I—" She gave him that look. That laser-eyed you-will-say-yes-if-you-know-what's-good-for-you stare. "—would be happy to."

Mrs. Crane beamed. "Thank you, Noah. You and Del were always such good friends. I'm sure he'll be glad to see you."

Noah's strained smile made his face hurt. Was she deliberately needling him, or did she really not know? If Del wanted to see him, he could have called or texted sometime in the last five years.

Maybe she assumed anything between Noah and her son was long forgotten, as it should be after all this time. But no matter how much Noah tried to forget Del, he hadn't been able to, especially when he was the one who'd stayed behind in Anticipation, Wyoming, population nowhere near enough.

"You're welcome. I'll need to get his flight information so I can check and see if it's on time."

"Oh, yes," Mrs. Crane said. "And you'll need Delford's phone number, or do you still have it?"

He almost said no, but this whole thing already had so much potential for humiliation it didn't really matter. "Has it changed since he left?"

"No."

"Then I still have it." Perfect. He was exposed as utterly pathetic.

"Oh good."

Noah's mother produced a piece of paper, and Mrs. Crane wrote down the flight information. He refrained from mentioning how much easier it would be to type the flight number into a note on his phone.

When Mrs. Crane left, Noah glanced around the bakery. All the morning customers seemed content at their tables with coffee and electronic devices or an actual human friend.

“May I see you in the kitchen?” he asked his mother, barely keeping his voice level.

“Noah, I hope you’re not going to be—”

“In. The. Kitchen.”

She sighed before turning and pushing through the swinging door.

“What were you thinking out there?” he asked once the door closed behind them.

“That you’re going to have to see Del sooner or later. Now it will happen right away, and you’ll get over any awkwardness quickly so it’s not hanging over you.”

Did she really think it would be that simple? “Mom, we’re going to be stuck in a car for almost two hours, and that’s if the weather holds.”

She sighed. “I guess I didn’t really think about that part.”

He narrowed his eyes. “You’re not thinking about matchmaking, are you? Do you remember what I was like after he left?”

“Of course I do. I had to do all the baking for days.”

“Oh my God, Mom.” Noah scrubbed a hand over his face. She clearly didn’t understand that his insides felt like they were rearranging themselves.

“I’m teasing. You were devastated, but he’s probably changed a lot, and even though you haven’t—”

“If you say I haven’t changed just because I chose to stay here, I’ll call Mrs. Crane and tell her she’ll have to find someone else.”

“I wasn’t going to say that. You’ve certainly changed.”

She was using her delivering-bad-news tone. “Are you saying it’s for the worse?”

“Not necessarily, but you have become a bit set in your ways.”

“Mom.”

"And you haven't exactly had much dating experience."

He hated how right she was, though it wasn't like he had many options considering the nonexistent pool of gay men in Smaller Than Smallville. Of course, it had been months—okay, maybe over a year—since he'd bothered going to Casper or Billings where he might have a chance of meeting someone. Hell, it had been months since he'd even gone to Sheridan for more than groceries or a movie. And yes, he'd chosen to stay in Anticipation. His mom didn't have any family close by. His father had run off, never to be seen again, when he was thirteen. A year later, his mom had decided they needed a major change, so she'd bought Main Street Bakery, and they'd been baking together ever since.

His mom didn't say anything else, just stared at him until he relented.

"Fine. You have a point, but pushing me toward Del is a terrible idea."

"Forcing you to clear the air with him when he'll be back here for who knows how long isn't. Even if I wasn't worried about you, I don't want to have to put up with you being a bitch every day because you're afraid he's going to walk in here and ask to see you."

"Mom!"

"Don't act like you won't be."

Noah sighed. "Why is he moving back, anyway?"

His mom shrugged. "I don't know, and Ada either isn't saying, or she doesn't know either."

"He won't stay. He hates it here."

"He hated it here when he was a kid. He might feel differently now."

Noah doubted that. Except for riding, Del had hated basically everything about Anticipation, and he hadn't thought a gay man could be out here. Noah couldn't believe he had to drive Del all the way home from Casper. "This is going to be torture."

His mom patted his shoulder. "You'll be fine."

"Stop being so optimistic."

"Stop borrowing trouble."

He narrowed his eyes at her. They were never going to agree on the line between pessimism and practicality. "You owe me."

She gave him an overly sweet smile. "If you say so. What can I do to make it even?"

"Nothing, but how about you run the front counter during the morning rush tomorrow? And I'll hide in the back." His mother always managed to have something that desperately needed her attention in the kitchen whenever customers began pouring in for their morning coffee, and she always enlisted the help of any other employees who were there. Thus, Noah ended up stuck at the register, which he hated. He was almost certain his mom did it to force him to interact more. Why couldn't she just leave his introverted self alone?

"Deal. I'll even do it for the rest of the week. You should pick out something to take to Del. He'll surely be hungry when he lands, and he probably hasn't had anything as good as your pie since he left."

Noah looked at the baked goods case. There was a cherry pie there, and it was amazing, but pie wasn't going to send the right message. Pie was something you made for someone you cared deeply for, not something you brought to a man who'd become less than an acquaintance.

He looked over his other options. He could take chocolate chip cookies, but that was too basic, like he was trying to be impersonal. "I'll pack up some of the brownies I just made."

His mother smiled. "Excellent choice. Why don't you go ahead and take off after you do that? You could go on to

Casper and have some fun while you wait for Del's plane to get in."

Noah tried to remember what people did for fun. "Like what?"

His mother sighed. "Shop. Go to a movie. Try a new restaurant."

All things that would be more exciting if he weren't on his own. He considered asking his friend, David, to come along with him, but he was fairly sure David was leading a hike that day. And he didn't really want a witness for his reunion with Del, not even one who was as understanding a friend as David. But his mother looked so determined that he just said thanks and hugged her. He'd figure out something to do.

TWO

Del clasped his hands together to keep from reaching for Clarice's shoes. He could do this. He could wait patiently for her to put them on herself. The alternative involved a lot of tears—probably a full-blown tantrum—and would possibly end up with them right back where they were now. But as he watched her push her foot partway into a shoe, then glance at him, then push her foot in a little more, then stop to trace the pictures of cupcakes on her tights, he thought he might scream.

Finally, she got both shoes on her feet, the wrong feet, but she didn't seem to care, and he didn't feel like arguing again. If she liked them that way, then fine. All he needed was for her feet to be covered for the trip to the airport, and it wasn't like anyone would care what a three-year-old was dressed like.

"Daddy, is Mommy still in heaven?"

Her words knocked the breath out of him, and he leaned back, needing the support of the wall. How could he be worried about shoes when she was still trying to process losing her mom? "Yes, she is."

"And she has to stay there?"

He nodded. "That's right. Once you go to heaven, you have to stay."

"But it's nice there, right?"

"It's very nice there." He hoped he was saying the right things, doing the right things. He would do anything to help her put her world back together.

"Okay. Can we go see horses now?" She practically bounced off the floor.

Del had mostly gotten used to her ability to move from one topic to another, and from sadness or anger to happiness in a single second, but sometimes it still shocked him. He forced himself to return her smile even though his mind was reeling with all the contradictory advice on grieving children he'd received over the last few months. Fortunately, it seemed he didn't need to say anything else now, so he scooped her up in his arms and squeezed her tight. "The horses are going to love you."

She giggled. "Of course they are, silly. Why wouldn't they?"

Why wouldn't they indeed? "Do you need to go potty before we leave?"

She shook her head.

Allen, his assistant—make that former assistant—had already taken his bags down to the waiting car. Del would still be working remotely for the same financial firm, but Allen would be assisting Del's replacement in the Chicago office. Allen's last task for him was overseeing the movers who would pack up the rest of their things and ship them out to Wyoming. Del glanced around the apartment to see if they were leaving anything they'd need for the next few weeks.

After one last lingering glance at the apartment, the kind of home he'd longed for since he was in his teens, the one he was abandoning for this sweet girl who was now his and his alone to care for, he closed the door behind them. They were halfway to the lobby when Clarice said, "I need to go potty."

He sighed. Of course she did. They rode back up. He waited as patiently as he was capable of while she used the bathroom. Then they headed down to the lobby once again.

This time they got all the way to the car before she looked around frantically. "Uni? Where's Uni?"

Fortunately, Del could solve this problem. He pulled her stuffed unicorn from his messenger bag where he'd stuck it while she used the bathroom.

She seized the worn, well-loved animal, and Del buckled her into her car seat.

"Thank you," he said, turning back to Allen.

"I'm glad I could help. Is there anything else you need?"

Del shook his head. "No. I'll let you know when I'm coming back."

"We're going to miss you." Allen's wistful voice made Del wonder, not for the first time, if he was interested in more than a working relationship, but even if that wasn't a disaster in the making, it was too late to find out now.

"I'll miss you too, as well as all this." He gestured toward the building, but Allen probably knew he didn't just mean the apartment but city life in general, the job he'd excelled at, his friends, everything.

"You know—"

Del held up a hand, not sure how many more times he could resist Allen encouraging him to stay. "Going back to Wyoming is best for Clarice. I have to put her first now." Even if he'd sworn he'd rather gouge his eyes out than move back to Anticipation.

Allen nodded. "I understand."

Del shook his hand and then sank into the car.

“Safe travels,” Allen said. The sound of the car door shutting seemed louder than it should. Del didn’t think he’d ever felt more suffocated in a vehicle, but his nerves weren’t important. He took Clarice’s hand in his and let the driver know they were ready to go.

A few moments later, his phone buzzed, and he pulled it from his jacket pocket. He read the text on the screen and then read it again. Perfect. The one person he dreaded seeing more than his family was going to be picking them up from the airport.

“Is Daddy sad?”

Sad. Such a small word to encompass how he felt when he thought of Noah. But he pushed away all his angst and made himself smile for Clarice’s sake. “No, Daddy’s not sad. But your grandma won’t be picking us up after all.”

“Is Grandma sad?”

“She won’t be after she meets you.” He prayed she wouldn’t be, anyway. The closer they got to seeing her, the more he started to realize his plan of surprising his parents with Clarice was probably completely stupid and exactly what he would have done in high school, as if simply deciding to go back home made him revert to the selfish kid he’d been.

“Me *and* Uni. She’ll love Uni.” Clarice hugged the animal tightly.

“Of course she will. But there’s a lot of snow, so she’s sending a… friend of mine to pick us up.” He seriously doubted Noah would consider them friends, but what could he call Noah, ‘the guy I used to be obsessed with who hates me now’?

“Does he have horses?”

“No. At least he didn’t the last time I saw him, but he loves to ride them.”

"Horses are the best."

Del squeezed her hand. "They are, and you're going to get to see them every day."

Having a chance to ride again was the one thing about returning to the ranch that he looked forward to. He'd missed the horses and Harvey, the foreman who'd understood him better than anyone else on the ranch. Harvey would adore Clarice and all her enthusiasm.

Clarice stared out the windows as buildings whizzed by. "See horses soon?"

"No, sweetie. It's a long trip."

"Like an hour?"

He sighed. This was going to be a long day. "Several hours. Remember we've got to get to the airport and then ride on a plane. After that we have to drive to my parents' house."

"An hour's a long time."

"It is, sweetie, but we'll be there eventually."

And then they'd be in the car with Noah. At least Clarice would help him keep up the conversation. When she wanted to, she could talk lightning-fast for so long Del couldn't believe her throat didn't get sore. With his luck, though, she'd fall asleep as soon as they got on the road. Then he'd be left in awkward silence with the man he'd never gotten over.

THREE

Noah paced back and forth in front of the carousels at baggage claim. When he wasn't busy glancing out the window to see how bad the snow looked, he was second-guessing his decision to come in and meet Del. He'd originally intended to wait in the cell phone lot until Del had his bags, but he'd decided having their reunion in public might be better. Besides, what was the point of having purchased new jeans—and changed into them in a coffee shop bathroom—as well as having gotten his hair cut if he wasn't going to let Del get a good look at him?

Oh God. What was he doing? He should not be worrying about what Del thought of him. He didn't want anything from the man. But at least if he were confident he looked good, he might do a better job of remaining aloof. Or maybe he should change back. He caught a glimpse of himself in one of the long windows that faced the parking lot. Damn, he'd never owned a pair of jeans that made his ass look this good. Nope. He wasn't changing. In fact, he might never take them off.

Finally his phone buzzed.

I just landed.

I'm at baggage claim, Noah responded.

See you soon.

The butterflies that had been fluttering around in Noah's stomach started a full-on aerial assault. In a few minutes he was going to see Del Crane for the first time in five years. They'd be stuck together in a car or—he glanced out the window—all night in a hotel. Snow was already blowing wildly, and he could tell it was the kind that piled up fast. The very real possibility that he was going to be stuck with Del all night started to weigh on him.

He checked his phone. Only two minutes had gone by since Del had texted, though it felt like it had been at least half an hour. He walked to the far end of baggage claim and back, then amused himself by looking at signs above the carousels to see if he could find Del's flight number. Once he located the right one, he turned to look toward the escalators.

And there he was: Delford Crane. The boy he'd longed for years ago. All grown up and yet exactly the same. That dark hair that flopped over his forehead, those wide shoulders, and the perfectly tailored clothes. Except… he was holding a little girl's hand. A little girl with the same color hair who looked exactly like him.

"Del?" It came out almost as a squeak.

He inclined his head, that same arrogant gesture Noah remembered so well. "Noah."

"Your mother didn't tell me you'd… have someone with you."

"That's because she didn't know." That rich voice of his ran right through Noah. "This is Clarice. She's my daughter."

Noah made a strangled sound, and Clarice moved closer to Del and hugged his leg.

Del Crane had a daughter. The world went very still and blurred at the edges. Only Del and Clarice were in focus.

Del took a step closer. "Noah? Are you all right?"

Del was talking to him, and he was standing there, mouth open, looking like an idiot.

"I'm sorry. I just had no idea. Your mom didn't tell me you had a child."

"She's never met Clarice."

"She—what?" It took a few moments for those words to sink in. And God, wasn't that just like Del. So much for thinking he might have changed. The prodigal son returns with a surprise adorable grandchild. He'd drink in the attention for days.

"How did you even…" Noah stopped himself from finishing the question, more than a little horrified at what he'd almost said. It wasn't any of his business how Del had ended up with a child, and it certainly wasn't something they should discuss in front of her.

Del sighed.

Wow, was that sound familiar. It was that same exasperated, no-one-knows-as-much-as-me sound Noah had heard so often in high school.

"It's a really long story."

Noah just bet it was. And obviously not one he was going to hear any time soon, if ever.

He started to run his hand through his hair, then remembered the stylist had gelled it into place. Why had his mom done this to him? And why had he actually begun to believe Del would be different? Though he had to admit when he looked past the perfectly groomed facade, Del looked far more worried and exhausted than arrogant. Probably just the stress of flying with a child. That certainly wasn't Del's style.

Noah turned his attention to Clarice. She was peeking at him now.

"Hi. I'm Noah."

She turned her face back into Del's leg, then slowly turned toward him again.

"I'm still here. You're going to ride in my car to see your—"

"Horses," she said.

He smiled. "Your grandparents do have some beautiful horses."

"A whole barn full."

Noah glanced at Del. He was looking down at Clarice, his face bright, open, and honest, reminding Noah of how he'd looked the night they finally gave in to all the tension sizzling between them.

Del bent down and scooped Clarice into his arms.

"I wish Grandma and Grandpa had a unicorn," she announced.

Del kissed the top of her head. "If they did, I would let you ride it as soon as we got there."

Noah's heart fluttered, which made him uneasy. He'd sworn to keep his distance from Del, because he was determined not to fall for him all over again. But this was a side of Del he'd never imagined. One he didn't know how to resist.

At that moment the bell over the conveyor began to ring and the belt jutted to life, signaling that luggage would appear soon. Del wasn't going to be able to grab their bags while holding Clarice.

"Tell me what to look for, and I'll grab it."

"There's mine," Clarice shrieked.

Noah didn't have to ask which one she meant. He saw a small suitcase with horses all over it. He stepped up to the belt, grabbed it, and set it at Del's feet.

"That big red one is ours too," Del said a few seconds later. Noah retrieved it as well.

"There's another one just like it and then Clarice's car seat, which has a purple plaid cover."

They stood waiting, watching the bags plop down onto the belt as Clarice kept up a litany of "not that one, not that one." Naturally, instead of coming out near the other bags, the other suitcase and the car seat were some of the last items to appear.

Once they finally had everything, Noah glanced around, wondering how they would get it all to the car. "Let's see if we can get this outside, and then I'll bring the car around."

Del looked relieved. "Thanks. I really do appreciate you driving all this way."

"It's no problem." They both knew that was a lie, but neither of them said anything else. Noah grabbed both of the big suitcases, and Del put Clarice down.

"Hold my hand, and we'll both pull your suitcase."

She clung to her bag with one hand and put the other on the handle of the suitcase. Del picked up her car seat in his other hand and followed Noah. As they got close to the door, Noah saw the snow swirling wildly, and he knew they weren't going to make it home.

Noah stopped and turned around. "The storm must've moved in quicker than expected. There's no way we'll make it back to Anticipation tonight."

"I reserved a hotel room when I saw there was a storm, so we wouldn't have to scramble for someplace to stay." Del didn't look any happier about the situation than Noah was.

"You really got a room just in case?" Noah supposed when you had the kind of money the Cranes did, wasting it on a hotel you might not use was no big deal.

"Once I saw the weather, I wanted to be sure we'd have a place to stay. Don't worry. It's a suite, so you'll have your own bed."

Of course Del had gotten a suite, probably the largest one. "That's great. And I wasn't worried. I could sleep on the floor or whatever. I was just really hoping to make it back tonight."

"Will your mom be okay with the bakery?"

Noah nodded. "There are a few people she can call to help out. She's the one who insisted I come get you, so she was obviously willing to take the risk of me getting stuck."

"Oh, okay." Del sounded sad, which made no sense. Maybe he was just tired.

"How close is the hotel?"

"It's right here at the airport, like half a mile away."

"Great. I'll take these suitcases and go get the car."

"Thanks," Del called after him.

THE DRIVE TO THE HOTEL WAS QUIET EXCEPT FOR CLARICE occasionally describing what she saw. Del kept thinking about how quick Noah was to point out that he hadn't volunteered to come get them, not that Del would have expected him to, but somehow it hurt that Noah was coerced into doing it.

You ran away and never called him. Did you think he'd be eager to see you?

I wanted him to leave with me, but he wouldn't.

All you were offering him was a chance to tag along on your dream, and you talked about it once. That night you ran, you didn't say a word.

Fuck. Noah is never going to forgive me.

Del was thankful when they pulled up at the hotel and he could push those thoughts aside. After they'd checked in, Del got Clarice set up with a video in one of the beds. He could tell she was getting sleepy, but as usual, she was fighting it. Maybe he'd get lucky, and she'd drift off.

"Are you hungry?" Noah asked when Del came back into the sitting area.

"I don't even know anymore. After getting Clarice through the airport and dealing with the delays and uncertainty, I hardly know if it's morning or night."

Noah looked at his phone. "It's nearly seven thirty. I brought you some brownies."

"You did? Really?" He'd thought he would have to sneak into Main Street Bakery when Noah wasn't working to be able to taste his baked goods again. If Noah had brought him brownies, then he didn't hate him like Del had feared.

Noah shrugged. "You know me, I'm always bringing people food, but I can go get something more solid if you need it."

"In a blizzard? Hell no, we're lucky to have gotten here safely."

"This? I drive in worse than this all the time. I was just worried about the roads farther up in the mountains."

"Oh right, I'm a city boy now, and you're the strong country boy who's too tough to let a blizzard stop him."

Noah snorted. "I wonder if you'll even be able to stay on a horse, city boy."

"Oh really. I'd be happy to race you."

"You couldn't beat me when we were eighteen. Why would you—" Noah froze. "Shi—Shoot." He winced. They both glanced toward the bedroom, but Clarice seemed to have fallen asleep.

"I didn't mean to bring that up," Noah added.

"Look, we have a past. We can't act like we didn't know each other."

"In the Biblical sense."

“Noah—”

He sighed, looking pained like he often had when Del was pushing for what he wanted. Even when he’d known he was pissing Noah off, he hadn’t been able to stop. “Fine, but if we’re not going to pretend, then we need to be completely honest.”

Del bristled at his superior tone. “If we couldn’t be honest five years ago, it’s not going to be any easier now.”

“I was honest with you.”

“Were you? Completely?”

Noah glanced away. “I was as honest as I could stand to be. We were still basically kids.” Del could almost hear the “or at least you were” tacked onto the end.

“You’re right. I wasn’t ready to face who I was. I was too much of a coward. Is that what you want me to say?”

Noah’s expression softened, and he shook his head. “No, because I don’t think you are. No coward would survive a flight with a—how old is Clarice?”

“She’s three.”

“With a three-year-old girl. And I can tell how much you love her.”

“Thank you.” The praise sent warmth through Del. He hoped he could be a good dad to Clarice, but every day he worried he was fucking it up. He turned away and picked up the room service menu. “I’ll order something for us, okay? And then I want those brownies.”

“Yeah, sure. You know what I like.”

“Do I?”

Noah nodded. “You do.”

FOUR

While Del called in their order, Noah took the opportunity to use the bathroom. When he came out, Del was looking out at the snow, his forehead pressed against the window and his lips forming a hard line.

Noah longed to touch him and see if he could dissolve some of that tension, but only because Del so clearly needed comfort. Noah wasn't stupid. He knew better than to think there could be more between them. Sooner or later, Del would run again. But right then, he wanted to soothe Del with a back rub like he'd often done years ago when they'd pretended to only be friends. Noah might not know what had happened to bring Del back to Wyoming, but he knew Del was in pain.

"I know what you probably think of me," Del said, his voice stark.

Did he think Noah was judging him for sleeping with a woman? For having been careless? For hiding Clarice? Okay, maybe he was judging Del a little for hiding her, but he seemed to be doing everything he could to make her happy.

How could he judge a man for that? "I really don't think you do."

Del turned and faced him. "I'm gay. I'm not in denial about it. That's not why I left."

"I remember very clearly why you left." Del might not have been in denial, but he didn't want to be gay in a town like Anticipation. And as much as it had hurt, Noah couldn't really blame him for that. It was the fact that he'd cut off all contact that had hurt the most.

"No. You don't." The pain in Del's eyes was so stark it made Noah ache.

"You wanted more than what you could have here, and you had every right to." Noah was shocked he'd been able to say those words without his voice breaking. If nothing else, that proved he'd changed in the last few years.

"Amy—Clarice's mother—and I were both drunk the night it happened."

Noah wasn't prepared for Del's confession. He'd intended to ask Del to sit down, but those words had him rooted to the spot, unable to speak and unsure if he wanted Del to go on or not.

"We were both miserable and trying to cheer each other up." He kept his voice low, barely a whisper. "Neither of us expected this to happen. She was moving the next day, and when she found out she was pregnant, she decided not to tell me."

"Did she think you'd be angry?"

"Not exactly. She was scared and confused, but she wanted to have the baby. I think mostly she worried I'd talk her out of it." He paced in front of the window. "I wouldn't have."

He sounded so sincere. Noah could tell it was important

to Del that Noah believed him. “I know you wouldn’t. When did you find out?”

“After Clarice was born. Amy called me. They were living in San Diego, so I couldn’t see Clarice often, but I visited as much as I could. I wanted her to know me.”

His voice cracked, and Noah could hardly believe he’d thought Del hadn’t changed. This was certainly not the man who’d stopped talking to him when Noah refused to follow after him like a puppy.

“But you didn’t tell your parents?”

Del shook his head. “I know I should have, but we hardly ever talked. Clarice became this wonderful secret, but I can’t keep her from them anymore, because now… because Amy…”

Del’s voice cracked, and Noah knew what was coming. He wanted to be wrong, but Del’s eyes were closed, squeezed tight, his whole body rigid. Noah’s mom had said Del was *moving* back, not just visiting.

Finally, he reached out and stroked Del’s back like he’d wanted to earlier. “You don’t have to say any more if you don’t want to.”

“I’m going to have to repeat it all God knows how many times. Everyone back home will expect the whole story.”

Del was right, but he didn’t have to be the one to tell it. “Once a few people know, the story will spread on its own. But if you’re worried people won’t get it right, I’ll tell them for you.”

Del looked up at him. “Why?”

“Why would I tell people?”

“No, why are you being nice to me?”

Noah frowned. “I’m not going to pretend it was easy after you left, but do you really think I’d want you to suffer when I could help?”

Del reached for his hand. Noah laced their fingers together and pulled him toward the couch.

"I cared for Amy," Del said after they were seated. "I didn't love her romantically, and we were never really together, but I cared about her as a good friend. And then… she was gone. Hit by a car. Dead on impact."

Noah squeezed his hand, not knowing what to say. He held back the standard "at least she didn't suffer" remark. Sure, that would have been worse, but her being dead sucked, and no social nicety was going to make it better. Finally, he simply said, "I'm so sorry."

"Yeah, me too."

"So you have custody of Clarice now?" Noah asked.

"I'm so scared I'm going to fuck it up." Del pressed his free hand against his eyes, and his whole body started to shake.

Noah couldn't stand seeing him so broken. He'd been worried he'd be drawn in by the sheer beauty and presence of Del, but he'd never anticipated Del needing him like this. Del stiffened at first when Noah pulled him into his arms, but as Noah ran a hand up and down his back, he surrendered, resting his head on Noah's shoulder until his tears soaked through Noah's shirt.

That morning, Noah had dreaded Del trying to distance himself with sarcasm or complaints during their drive home. He would never have imagined he'd be sitting in a posh hotel room—or one as posh as Casper got—with a tiny girl dozing in the bed while Del literally cried on his shoulder.

The blizzard was turning out to be a blessing. Del needed a chance to talk things through with someone before seeing his family, because as soon as he walked into that ranch house with Clarice, gossip would start to spread, and the questions would come at him fast and sharp.

A few moments later, Del pulled away and wiped his eyes.

"Wow. I'm… This is really embarrassing."

Noah shook his head. "You have every right to grieve."

"I've tried to stay strong for Clarice, but sometimes it's so hard."

"I think it's okay for her to know you miss her mom, that you cared for her, and it hurt you to lose her."

"I don't want to make her even sadder or have her think she needs to take care of me."

Noah ached for him, but this wasn't the time to argue about healthy grieving, and Del knew Clarice much better than he did.

"Are you really moving back to Anticipation? You and Clarice?"

Del nodded. "I was living in the financial district in Chicago. There were hardly any kids in my building, and no place for Clarice to play. I hired a nanny, but I hated never getting to see Clarice because I was working all the time. That's not what I want for her."

"But isn't that the life you always wished for as a kid?"

Del frowned. "Yeah, but Clarice loves being outside, and at the ranch she can spend as much time with the horses as she likes."

"Won't you be miserable here, though? You could just visit often."

Del sighed. "I'll stay out of your way as much as possible."

"No, that's not what I meant."

"It's okay. I appreciate you coming to get us."

"Del, stop." He was still as infuriating as he'd been in high school. "You're arguing to distance yourself from me just like you always did."

"Look, I know you don't agree with my choices, but—"

"I'm worried about you, and you'd get that if you weren't so damn stubborn."

"*I'm* stubborn?"

"Fine. We both are, but you said you were miserable here; I don't want you to feel that way now."

They stared at each other. Noah hadn't realized how close they'd gotten. He could feel the heat of Del's leg against his own. Del licked his lips and suddenly Noah couldn't remember what he'd been about to say. Del had him mesmerized. His hair was much shorter than when they'd last been together. It looked good on him, allowing his sharp cheekbones and full mouth to draw Noah's attention. He wanted to touch Del, to kiss him, to push him back until he could press him down into the couch. It was a good thing Clarice was in the next room, because otherwise, he wouldn't be able to trust his self-control.

"I chose to come back."

The words startled Noah.

"I'm not going to run away. I'm going to find a way to make it work, because I think it's best for Clarice. As long as she's happy, I'll be fine."

"All right." Noah hoped that was true.

"Maybe I won't hate it quite so much, and at least I'll get to ride every day."

"And Clarice will have lots of horses to love."

Del smiled. "Those horses have no idea what's coming."

"She's going to have so much fun, and I meant what I said. I'll do what I can to make people leave you alone. No matter what happened between us before you left, Clarice deserves a good start in Anticipation."

"What about me?"

Noah gave him an assessing glance. "I haven't decided about you yet."

"NO?" DEL HELD HIS GAZE, SURE HE COULD SEE THE flutter of Noah's pulse in his neck.

He leaned closer and breathed in the smell of sunshine and fresh bread. How did Noah always still smell like a bakery when he'd been away from work for hours? He held Noah's pale-blue gaze, but he couldn't help thinking about his strong hands, the way they could manipulate dough, the way they'd felt skimming over Del's bare flesh. Those months were still so clear in his memory, like it had happened a few days ago. And despite all their clumsiness and all the fear and uncertainty between them, it was still the best damn sex Del had ever had and the only time he'd truly connected with the man he was with.

He brushed a hand over Noah's cheek, enjoying the scrape of stubble. He shouldn't be doing this, especially with Clarice in the next room, and yet it felt so right.

"Del, what are you…?" Noah's words were low and rough. He was feeling this too, even though he held himself stiffly.

Del slid his hand down and cupped the back of Noah's neck. "Can I—"

Knock. Knock. Knock.

"The food is here," Noah whispered, his eyes wide, his chest rising and falling rapidly.

Del nodded and pulled back. As he crossed the room on shaky legs, he wondered if Noah would have let Del kiss him. Would there be another chance to find out? Should there be?

He took the tray of food and tipped the man who'd

brought it. Clarice called just as he set the tray on the table. "Daddy! The video's stuck!" So much for her being exhausted enough to stay asleep.

"If you want to get the food set up, I'll see if I can fix it," Noah said.

"Thanks." He got the sense Noah wanted to put some distance between them, which wasn't a bad idea. Not that Del was going to ravish him with Clarice awake and their food getting cold, but he needed to keep his distance so he could focus on getting settled, setting himself up to work remotely, and finding a preschool for Clarice so she could meet some other kids. He didn't have time for dating, even if Noah wanted him, even if Del had the courage to date a man in his hometown.

He found plates and utensils in the room's kitchenette and set the table. After opening up the food, he stepped into the bedroom. Noah was stretched out next to Clarice, who was giggling madly as he narrated whatever was happening on screen.

"There. Press on that one," Noah said, pointing at the screen.

She cackled as she smushed her finger against the tablet harder than was necessary.

Del winced. "Be careful."

"Daaaaaaddy, I know what I'm doing."

"Clarice, your dad's right. If we break it, we can't play with the fish anymore."

"More fish!" She nudged Noah with the tablet.

"I think it's time to eat dinner."

"Then more fish?"

"If that's okay with your dad." Noah looked over at him, and Del couldn't breathe. Noah was just as beautiful as he'd always been and seeing him with Clarice, both of them so happy, was too much for Del.

Finally he found his voice. "You're playing Glitter Fish?"

Clarice nodded vigorously. "Noah is better at it than you."

"Is he, now?" Del glanced at Noah who shrugged, giving Del the smirk that had done wicked things to him back in high school.

"You never catch the fish, Daddy."

He huffed dramatically as if he were incredibly offended. "Come eat, and then yes, you and Master Player Noah can enjoy a few more games before bedtime."

Amazingly, Clarice accepted the hotel's version of mac and cheese, and she loved Noah's brownies as much as Del did. She didn't even scrape off the coffee-flavored frosting. But the second Noah took the last bite of his dessert, she tugged on his arm to pull him back to their game.

Del opened his own tablet. He was exhausted, but he needed to take care of some emails and make some notes on the one project he hadn't delegated to someone else. He didn't get very far, though; Noah's and Clarice's shrieks and laughter pulled his attention back to the bedroom. After sending a few messages, he gave up and walked over to stand in the doorway and watch them. Seeing Noah like that—playful, carefree, not at all the serious man he'd been earlier in the evening—made his chest tighten. What would it be like to have a man like that in his life?

Be serious. You don't want "a man like that"; you want Noah.

It had been so long since they'd seen each other. How was he still so infatuated? But hardly a day had gone by that he hadn't thought of Noah in some way. Where would they be now if he hadn't been too scared and too damn arrogant to listen to Noah?

He truly had needed to get away from home, to experience something different than small-town Wyoming, but demanding that Noah join him and give up his own dreams… God, he'd been an asshole. He couldn't believe Noah was even willing to speak to him.

FIVE

By late morning the next day, the snow had tapered off and the main roads were cleared. After lunch at a pancake house—Clarice's choice because, apparently, she hadn't gotten enough breakfast food to satisfy her, despite Del ordering what looked like most of the room service menu—Noah determined that they should be able to make it back to Anticipation.

"We see horses now?" Clarice asked as they loaded the luggage into Noah's car.

"That's right, sweetie," Del said.

"And horses have snow too."

"They probably have even more than we have here," Noah said.

The drive wasn't at all what Noah had imagined the day before when he'd been dreading long, awkward silences. Clarice chattered almost constantly for the first hour until, finally, she gave in to Del's suggestion that she watch a video.

Noah glanced in the rearview mirror. Clarice had a serious expression on her face as she stared at the screen, and her over-the-ears headphones looked enormous on her, making her even more adorable than usual.

“Sorry,” Del said a few minutes later. “She can be a bit much.”

“I don’t mind.” And he truly didn’t. He was enjoying Clarice’s exuberance.

“You don’t have to say that.”

“No, really. She’s great. I…”

“What?” Del asked.

Noah wished he’d stayed quiet. “You know I’ve always wanted to have kids eventually.”

They’d shared their visions for the future years ago. Noah had wanted to get married and adopt at least one if not several children. Del hadn’t been interested in kids or family life, which was ironic as hell, especially since Noah felt less sure every year that he’d find someone to build a family with.

“I do remember.” Del’s voice was soft, almost wistful. “You’re really good with her. I think you’d be—”

“Don’t say it.”

“Noah, I’m not—”

He shook his head. “It’s not like I—”

“Like you what?” There was a harsh edge to Del’s voice now. Did he think Noah was going to mock him for how he’d ended up with Clarice?

“Have much chance of ever finding someone else who wants kids too.” Del didn’t say anything. Noah wished he’d never started this conversation. “I’m fuckin—” He glanced in the rearview mirror again. Thankfully Clarice was still engrossed in her movie. “—messing this all up. It’s just that seeing you care so much about Clarice, knowing you’re giving up what—”

“I wouldn’t give up for you?”

"God, Del. I never wanted you to give up on your dreams. That's why it was all so hard for me."

"I'm sorry for how I acted back then."

"Me too," Noah said. At the time he thought he'd done everything right, but he knew better now.

"You have nothing to apologize for," Del insisted.

"I could have tried to understand, tried to come up with a compromise that—"

"No, I was awful and arrogant, and the things I said…"

Noah was glad he had to keep his eyes on the road. The quiver in Del's voice tugged at his heart, but at least he couldn't see the soft, lost expression he was sure was on Del's face. That look could make Noah do almost anything for him.

He was already falling for Del all over again, but he couldn't trust him to stay. Yes, he'd said Clarice would be happier here, but after living in Chicago, working for a big financial firm, could he really be happy in a town that didn't even have a Starbucks or its own movie theater?

They didn't say much for the rest of the drive. Del seemed to be dozing, and Noah didn't disturb him until they were almost to his family's ranch.

"Del?" No response. "Del!" When he still didn't wake, Noah reached over and jostled his shoulder. He pulled his hand back quickly. The feel of firm muscle made Noah wish there'd be more touching in their future.

"Sorry," Del said. "I didn't sleep very well last night."

"Did Clarice keep you up?" The two of them had shared the bed where Del had initially settled Clarice.

"No, she was so exhausted she hardly stirred. I just couldn't get my mind to quiet down." Noah wasn't surprised Del had a lot on his mind.

"We're almost there. I thought you'd want to be wide awake for your return."

Del blew out a long breath. "Yeah, that would be best."

"Horses!" Clarice yelled. She'd taken off her headphones and was bouncing as hard as she could while restrained in a car seat. "My horses?"

"No, those aren't your grandparents' horses, but they belong to our neighbor."

"Can I meet them too?"

"Maybe. Probably."

Rob Carter had recently purchased the neighboring ranch. He hadn't spent much time in Anticipation yet, but when Noah had met him, he'd seemed friendly. He bet Clarice would charm him easily. But before she could meet Rob's horses, she had to meet her grandparents. Noah still couldn't believe Del hadn't told them about her. "Don't you think you ought to call your mom and…" He wasn't sure what he should say in front of Clarice.

"I waited this long; I might as well keep it a surprise."

"I don't know, Del."

"Look, I know you think I'm an as—a not smart person."

"Daddy's very smart." A good reminder that she was listening to everything now. "Most of the time."

Noah laughed. "She keeping you humble?"

"Yeah, she does a great job of that. I think my parents will like the surprise. I… hope they will."

"Yeah, me too."

A few moments later, they turned into the driveway of Crane Acres.

"Why don't you come in with us?" Del said, the words seeming to burst from him.

"To see your parents?"

"Yes." Del's voice shook, and part of Noah wanted to do

what he asked. But his being there would only make things more awkward, wouldn't it?

"This is your reunion with them, and their chance to meet Clarice. I shouldn't intrude on that."

"You have to show me the horses," Clarice said.

Shit, how was he supposed to resist both of them? His mother was going to owe him a hell of a lot more than working the morning rush for this.

"Noah probably needs to work, sweetie. He's already done us a big favor by driving all that way to pick us up."

Damn Del for sounding so resigned.

"I want him to stay," Clarice shrieked. Great. Noah was going to be the cause of a tantrum right as they got to Del's house.

"Clarice," Del warned.

"I like him. He said he'd make me a special cupcake."

Noah glanced over at Del. "I hope that's okay."

Del laid a hand on his leg, and Noah nearly jumped. "It's fine. More than fine."

"Pleeeeeease, Noah," Clarice begged.

Noah decided maybe he shouldn't be a dad after all, because he had no idea how to say no to a little kid. "I think your grandparents will want some time with just you and your dad, but I could come visit another day." Except he'd sworn he'd keep his distance after he brought Del home.

"No!" she shouted.

Del's hand was still on him, and Noah felt him tense as he stopped the car by the door that led into the Crane's mudroom.

"Noah?"

"Yes?"

"I know I have no right to ask, but please stay. It would…

mean a lot to me." He sounded almost as shaky as he had before he'd ended up sobbing on Noah's shoulder.

"Things aren't going to be like they were with us."

Del cleared his throat. "I know. I'm sorry. I shouldn't have—"

Noah started to speak again, but Del stepped out of the car and opened Clarice's door. When he reached in to undo Clarice's car seat straps, she pushed his hand away. "I stay with Noah."

"Clarice, Noah needs to go."

She kicked her feet and pushed his hand away again.

Noah got out, circled the car, and laid a hand on Del's shoulder. "I'll stay. For as long as you need me."

He could tell himself he was doing this for Clarice, but he wasn't that deep in denial. Everything he'd felt for Del, all the things he'd pushed into his subconscious, had risen to the surface the moment he'd seen his former friend. And now, for better or worse, he wasn't going to walk away.

SIX

"I want Noah to get me out," Clarice demanded.

Del started to step away, but Noah squeezed his shoulder. "No, that's your dad's job. He knows how to work all those straps. I'll go with you to meet the horses, though."

"You will?"

"Yes."

She narrowed her eyes and studied him. "Promise?"

"I promise."

"Okay." She jabbed at the release button, trying to free herself. Del helped her, then scooped her out of her seat.

"Would you grab the backpack?" he asked Noah. "We can leave the rest of the bags. Mom will send someone to get them."

Noah rolled his eyes just like he would have years ago. He'd never understood how casually Del accepted that his family had servants to take care of them, though he'd sure loved Ella's cooking. At least he still got to see her most Sunday mornings at church.

Noah squeezed Del's shoulder again, and that small contact sent shivers through him. "It's going to be fine."

"No, I don't think it is."

"Then you'll pick up the pieces and figure out what to do with them."

"Is that what you did?" The words "when I left" hung in the air.

Noah nodded sharply. "Yes." Of course, that was a total lie. He'd wallowed in misery for months.

"Are you happy here?" Del asked.

Noah suspected Del was looking for reassurance or maybe absolution. "Do you need me to say yes?"

He shook his head. "I need you to tell me the truth."

The truth was too complicated for a simple answer. "I ask myself that most days, and the answer is yes and no."

The door opened then, and Del's mother stared at them. His father stood behind her, leaning heavily on a single crutch. Clarice turned and buried her face in Del's shoulder.

Please let this go okay, Noah prayed. He worried his presence would ultimately make it worse, but no way was he leaving after he'd promised to stay. For Clarice. He was staying for her, not because Del turned those sad, beautiful eyes on him.

He'd keep telling himself that. Maybe, eventually, he'd believe it was true.

"Delford." Mr. Crane inclined his head toward his son.

"Hi Dad, Mom."

"Hello, son," Mrs. Crane said.

Del was pale. He looked terrified. Noah contemplated speaking up, but it wasn't his place to tell the Cranes that this little girl currently clutching her stuffed unicorn so hard her knuckles were white was their granddaughter. *Oh, Del. Why did you go for the dramatic entry?*

Del whispered something to Clarice, and she shook her head fiercely.

"This is Clarice," Del said. "She's my daughter."

He said the word firmly as if expecting an argument.

His mother's eyebrows shot up. "Your daughter?"

She used the prim, haughty tone Noah was most familiar with. He hurt for Del.

"And your granddaughter."

"Can't you see she looks just like him, Ada?" his father asked.

She frowned at him. "Well, of course I can, but it's just a shock."

Del turned to Noah, a pleading look in his eyes. This was obviously not going the way he'd expected.

The desire to rescue him nearly took Noah's breath. No, to rescue Clarice. That's what it was. She needed his help. "Clarice is really tired. She didn't sleep well in the hotel last night. Maybe Del could take her up to her room to rest for a while."

Ada Crane glared at him, and he knew he'd said the wrong thing.

"Horses," Clarice said, looking at him and not at her grandparents. "You said you'd take me."

"She wants to see the horses," Del said as if there were any chance they hadn't understood.

"I…" His mother paused. Noah had never seen her lack for words. "I just can't believe you haven't introduced us before."

His dad took some halting steps backward. "Ada, let them in. They've got to be freezing."

They joined his parents in the foyer. Was it even more opulent than it had been the last time Noah was there?

Clarice peeked at her grandparents and Mrs. Crane apparently took that as a signal. "Welcome, Clarice. Would you like something to eat or drink?"

Clarice shook her head and returned to burying her face in Del's shoulder.

His dad started to say something, then stopped. It was clear he had no idea how to handle this situation.

"Clarice." Del turned his head to whisper to her. "Can you say hello to your grandparents?"

She shook her head again.

When Del looked up, Noah mouthed, "Should I take her?"

"Would it be all right if Noah walked out to the barn with her?" Del asked his parents.

His mother gave Noah a skeptical look.

"You may have forgotten, Mrs. Crane, but I used to babysit in high school."

She gave a brittle laugh. "Oh, that's right. I always thought it was so strange, a boy wanting to do that."

Apparently even gay boys weren't supposed to be good with children.

He laid a hand on Clarice's back. "Do you want to go to the barn with me?"

She pushed her hair back so she could look at him. "Horses?"

"Yes, to see the horses."

"Ok."

She reached for him, and he took her from Del. "Are you sure this is all right?" he asked Del, feeling strange talking in front of his parents like they weren't there, but needing the confirmation. "You don't need to be there?"

"I…" Noah could see he wanted to share that moment with his daughter, but he shook his head.

"How about if we just meet one of the horses? Then you can join us and introduce her to the others."

Clarice frowned at Noah, and he braced himself for an

argument, but she said, "Yes. One horse. Then Daddy comes."

Del smiled. "Thank you."

Noah nodded to Del's parents. "It's good to see the two of you. I hope your leg is getting better, Mr. Crane."

"It is. Thank you, Noah. I'll be getting around without this foul thing in no time." He jabbed the crutch into the floor for emphasis. "How have you been doing? I've sure enjoyed all the treats Ada brings me from the bakery."

"I'm doing fine. The bakery's keeping me busy."

"It's good of you to help your mom out," Mrs. Crane said.

Noah suppressed a sigh. He did a lot more than help out, but there was no point in arguing, and he wasn't sure if that was a dig against him or Del or just her way of making conversation.

Del's father looked down at Clarice then, seeming more nervous than Clarice was, which Noah could guarantee would not help.

"Hi, there. Is that a horse you've got?"

She shook her head.

"May I pet it?"

She shook it again harder. "Uni is mine."

He straightened back up. "So she's a unicorn."

"He's a unicorn."

At least Clarice was talking and Mr. Crane was making an effort with her.

"We don't have any unicorns here," Del's father said, "but we do have lots of horses."

Mr. Crane had always seemed so no-nonsense. It was odd to hear him talking about unicorns like they were real. Almost as odd as Del having a child.

"I like horses too," Clarice declared.

"Good. You'll like it here then."

"Noah," Mrs. Crane said. "Do you remember the way?"

"To the barn? I sure do."

"Go on with Noah, honey," Del said. "You're going to love the barn."

She rocked back and forth in Noah's arms as if trying to get him to giddy up. "Go. Go. Go."

"All right, wiggleworm."

Noah set Clarice down once they stepped into the mudroom. "Do you need help with your boots?"

"No." She shook her head vigorously. "I do it self."

"Well, I'm happy to hear that because I'm having trouble with mine." He had to fight the laces to pick out a knot they'd gotten into when he'd taken them off hurriedly.

When he finally got himself sorted out, Clarice was looking at her boots with a very serious expression.

"Is something wrong?"

"They won't tell me which one goes on this foot."

"Ah, yes. Boots are especially stubborn that way. May I take a look?"

She sighed dramatically. "I suppose."

He helped her sort out the problem, and they made the trek to the barn. The snow was deeper than her boots in places, so she gave in to letting Noah carry her.

When he set her down in the door of the barn, her eyes went wide. "It's huge."

"It's the largest barn in the area, as far as I know."

"And it's Daddy's?"

"Well, it belongs to your grandparents mostly, but yeah, I guess it's partly his too."

"Wow. Can I sleep here?"

The barn was heated, but he doubted it would be the right place for a little girl to spend the night. "I'm not sure your dad would think that was a good idea."

She huffed.

"But there's a nice hayloft for sitting and reading."

"There is?"

Noah grinned. "Of course. But first, let's—"

"Del? Is that you?"

Harvey, the Crane's foreman, came around the corner. "Noah! It's been way too long since you've been in this barn."

"It has," he agreed. "How are you doing?"

"I'm about as well as can be expected for an old man."

Noah raised his brows. "You can't be that old."

"Tell that to my wife."

Noah snickered. "I'll try to remember that next time I see her."

"Who is this?" Harvey asked, looking at Clarice. "Have you made a new friend I didn't know about?"

"This is Clarice. She's Del's daughter."

"Del's…? Oh my. I guess there must be a story there."

"There is. But I'll let him tell it."

"My mommy died," Clarice said.

The way she said it so matter-of-factly shook Noah. He had to look away for a moment and take a deep breath. Thank God Del had been there for her. Every time Noah had gotten annoyed with him since they'd been reunited, he'd tried to remember what Del must have gone through in the last few months. Noah still had so many questions about what had happened, but knowing how many others would pry, he hadn't wanted to push for more details.

"Del and his parents needed some time," Noah told Harvey. "So I brought Clarice out here."

Harvey nodded. "I bet they did. They haven't been keeping this a secret from me, have they?"

Noah shook his head. “They just met Clarice for the first time too.”

“Grandma made a face like she’d eaten sour gummy worms.”

Noah wanted to say that her grandmother often made that face, but he restrained himself.

“I’m sure she was just surprised and didn’t know how to react,” Harvey said.

“Clarice wants to meet the horses, but I promised Del I would just introduce her to one of them, and he could be here for the rest.”

“All right. Let’s meet Moon Pie. You won’t remember her, Noah. She’s a Shetland pony we just acquired from a rescue about six months ago. She’s very sociable, sweeter than a lot of little ponies. Most of them act like they’ve got something to prove.”

“I didn’t know you got horses from a rescue center,” Noah said.

“Well, the Cranes have been kind enough to let me do some fostering and even to let a few of the horses live here permanently. It’s something I’ve always wanted to do. Moon Pie is the perfect size for Clarice, so I’m really glad we have her.”

Noah nodded. Horses were larger than a lot of people realized until they were up close with one. They could be rather intimidating.

Harvey bent down so he was closer to Clarice’s level. “Clarice, I’m Harvey, and I’m in charge of things in the barn. I’ve known your father all his life.”

“Was he bad when he was my age?”

Harvey laughed. “He had his moments.”

“He said he loved horses just like me.”

"That's true. And he's a good rider. Even when he was as small as you, he took good care of the horses."

"I'm not small. I just haven't had a chance to get all growed up yet."

"Of course you haven't. You'll need several more years for that. How old are you? Four?"

She held up three fingers.

"Ah. Three is an excellent age."

Clarice beamed.

"Would you like to meet Moon Pie? He loves children and treats, but he doesn't always like to listen."

"Like me."

"You don't like to listen?" Harvey asked.

"Not when it's nap time or time for Daddy to go to work."

"Hmmm. I can understand that except now that I'm old, I love naps."

"Daddy likes naps. He's old too."

Noah snickered and Harvey bit his lip, like he was trying to hold in a burst of laughter.

"What treats do they like?" Clarice asked. "I like candy."

Harvey nodded. "Me too, but to a horse, a carrot or an apple is a treat."

Clarice frowned. "I only eat carrots when Daddy makes me."

"Well, Moon Pie thinks carrots are the best things ever." Harvey handed her two carrots, and she clutched them tightly in her small hand.

"I think the bestest thing is chocolate."

"I agree," Noah said. "But I also like carrots."

She held one of them out to him.

"Oh, I don't need one now. Let's save it for Moon Pie."

"Okay."

"Are you ready to meet her?" Harvey asked.

"Yes. Right now," Clarice insisted.

"Follow me, then."

Clarice held Uni out toward Noah. "You have to hold him. He might get scared."

"Oh." His breath caught as he took the worn stuffed animal. He didn't think Clarice trusted many people with her precious Uni. She'd rarely let go of him since Noah had met her.

"I promise to keep him safe."

She glared at him. "You better."

He bowed low. "I shall guard his life with my own, Your Highness."

She nodded just like a queen accepting the service of a knight.

Then she turned to follow Harvey.

Noah hugged the stuffed animal tight as they proceeded through the barn. He'd told himself he was going to stay away from Del, and now he'd become a confidant of Del's daughter—OMG, Del had a daughter. And he'd ended up right back where he'd been senior year, helping Del navigate his family and being the one to prop him up when his impulsiveness got him into trouble. Noah should probably be furious or nervous that Del had sucked him back into his world so fast. Instead, he felt hopeful and lighter than he had in a while. Hope was a dangerous emotion. He'd learned that in the months after Del fled town. But maybe, just maybe, it was time to try it again.

SEVEN

After Del had greeted Ella, the woman who'd been his family's housekeeper for much of his life, she got him a cup of coffee and a piece of cake. Then he and his parents sat down in the den.

"Delford, what's going on?" his mother asked.

"Please call me Del."

"This is hardly the time to worry about nicknames."

It would apparently never be the time, since she hadn't yet bothered to stop using his full name despite him asking her to for ten years. He started to say that but stopped himself in time. For once, she was right. This wasn't the time to push that particular issue. Instead, he paused long enough to take a sip of coffee, and then said, "I'm sorry I didn't tell you about Clarice. I'll try to explain why."

"I do think you owe us that," his father said.

His mother shook her head. "Whatever the explanation, I doubt it can make up for you not telling us we have a granddaughter."

Del hated how right she was. He'd been an idiot at best and cruel at worst. "We've hardly talked for years."

"Through no fault of ours," his mother snapped.

She managed to make him feel like a teenager all over again: afraid, confused, knowing he was being a jerk but not sure how to change.

"I needed to get away from here, to be on my own." He was supposed to be talking about Clarice, not defending himself for running.

"So you said, but keeping a child from us… That's just…"

"I only saw her occasionally at first."

"Where's her mother?"

Del squeezed his eyes shut. He did not want to cry. Not now. How was this so different than he'd expected? "I thought you'd be happy."

"We are," his mother said. "Clarice is beautiful. And I can't wait to get to know her."

The weight on Del's chest lightened. At least none of their animosity would be taken out on Clarice.

"We're glad you're home," his father said. "We've missed you, but we just wish you'd told us about Clarice before now."

"I don't even have a room made up for her," his mom huffed.

"She won't mind that. She might want to stay with me anyway."

"Nonsense. She'll want her own room."

Del started to pick up his coffee then set it back down; his stomach was too unsettled. "She has nightmares, and I need to be there in case she wakes up. She hasn't slept well since she lost her mother."

His father frowned. "What happened, son?"

He knew his dad didn't just mean Amy's accident. "Her mother and I were good friends. We had a very brief relationship while we were both upset over various things in our lives and needed comfort."

His mother sniffed.

"I know you don't approve. I didn't expect you to—"

"Things happen," his father said. "But weren't you careful?"

"I wasn't. I should've been, but I can't ever regret Clarice." He'd been stunned and upset at first, but Clarice had taught him so much. He was a better person for knowing her.

"So?" his mother asked, and he realized he'd paused for too long.

"I didn't know Amy was pregnant. She called me after Clarice was born. They were living in California, so I flew out to meet her. Amy said it was up to me if I wanted to be a part of her life. I did. I wasn't going to let her grow up not knowing me and thinking I didn't want her. I saw her as often as I could. It wasn't much, but I loved being at least a small part of her life."

"Why didn't you let us know?" His mother's voice shook. Her polite hostess mask was completely gone.

"I didn't tell anybody, not even my closest friends in Chicago. I wasn't sure anyone would understand my relationship with Amy."

"Because you're gay?" his father asked.

He nodded. "And I still am, by the way."

His mother sputtered. "But you and Amy. You… You had a child."

He sighed. It was hard to explain. "The night with Amy was an aberration, not a sign that I'm actually bi or straight or something."

"You said it was a short-term relationship," his mother insisted.

It hurt that she seemed so hopeful he was straight after all.

"I was trying to avoid saying drunken one-night stand."

She sighed. "Oh."

He took another deep breath. "About nine months ago, Amy moved back to Chicago, and I started seeing Clarice more regularly and having her spend some weekends with me. Then Amy got hit by a car, and she was… gone. I assumed full custody of Clarice."

"What about Amy's parents?" his father asked. "Have they seen her?"

He shook his head. "Amy wasn't on speaking terms with them. They didn't even show up for the funeral."

"Well, that's just horrid," his mother said.

Del nodded. "It is. Her father's an alcoholic, and he made things hell for her and her mom, but her mom wouldn't leave him, so Amy got out as soon as she graduated from high school."

"I suppose having a family you didn't talk to was something you had in common."

"Ada," his father growled. "There's no call for—"

"I'm sorry. This is just…"

"A lot. I know," Del said, pretending her words hadn't hurt. "I shouldn't have handled things like I did."

"Well—" His mother paused. "Maybe we can put that behind us."

"I'd like that."

"So you've been raising Clarice on your own for months, and you're just now telling us?" his father asked.

"I was messed up at first. Just trying to survive."

"And you didn't think we could help?" his mother asked.

"I should have known you would. I should have called. Once I realized Clarice needed to get out of the city, and I needed more time for her, I thought it would be fun to surprise you. I was wrong."

"You were, but we... we..." His mother held out her arms, and he sagged against her, hugging her tight. "I love you, Del." She emphasized the nickname, clearly wanting him to notice.

His dad patted his back. "Me too, son."

When his mother finally let him go, he said, "Is it going to be a problem that I'm gay?"

"No, not if that's really what's best for you." She sounded resigned rather than happy, and her phrasing left a lot to be desired. Hopefully that would improve with time.

"It's going to be an issue for a lot of other people, though," his father added.

"Don't most people know?"

"We didn't go around broadcasting it," his father said. "But a lot do know, and others suspect."

His mother nodded. "And if you... Well, if..."

His father interrupted. "Son, I think your mother is trying to ask if you and Noah are together?"

He was really glad he'd stopped drinking his coffee, because he might have spewed it all over himself. "No. He's... No."

His mother studied him for a moment. "Were you together in high school?"

"Moooom. I don't want to talk about high school."

"Of course you don't."

His dad laid a hand on his mom's shoulder. "Ada, I'm sure Del's tired. Why don't we let him rest until dinner?"

"Actually, I need to go see how Clarice is doing in the barn."

"That's right. You wanted to see her with the horses," his father said.

He nodded.

His mom sighed. "All right. Tell me what Clarice likes to

eat. I'll see if Ella can make some of her favorites for dinner. Maybe she'll feel more like talking to us once she's settled in."

"She will warm up and once she does, she's not going to stop talking."

His mother laughed. "Much like you at her age."

DEL STEPPED INTO THE BARN AND THE FIRST THING HE SAW was Clarice offering a carrot to a pony he hadn't seen before. Noah stood behind her, speaking encouraging words in a low voice and holding Uni tight against his chest. Del's breath caught, and he had to hold on to the doorframe to steady himself.

In that moment, he wanted Noah more than he ever had. This wasn't like his adolescent crush, that desire to possess the boy he'd wanted since the first moment he'd seen him. This was something stronger, purer, and far more frightening. He longed for a soft, comfortable love, something he doubted he could ever have. Would Noah even give him a chance?

He took a deep breath and forced himself to move, making his way across the barn. Noah turned, and Del tensed, waiting for his reaction. Del had begged—wow, he'd really, truly begged—Noah to stay and thrown him right into an awkward situation which Del's arrogant stupidity had made so much worse.

Noah didn't seem angry, though. He smiled, a slow curling of his lips, as if he were trying not to laugh. Then Del remembered he'd left his dress pants on and just pulled on boots to go out to the barn.

"Go ahead and laugh. I'm sure I look ridiculous."

Noah chuckled, a low, warm sound that Del wanted to

hear over and over. "Yeah, you do, but I think I like it."

That made Del's heart skip a beat. "Y-You do?"

Noah nodded. Then his expression turned more serious. "I hate that you weren't here to see Clarice meet Moon Pie."

"No, it's my own fault for not talking to my parents. If I couldn't be with her, you and Harvey are exactly who I'd choose."

"But you—"

"I screwed up. And I had to try and explain. It wasn't fair to make Clarice wait because of me." He paused, realizing how shaky his voice was. Talking to his parents had really rattled him.

"Are you okay?"

Del closed his eyes for a moment and swallowed, willing himself to be. "Yeah."

Noah raised his brow. "That didn't sound very—"

"Daddy!" Clarice shrieked, whirling around and reaching out her hand. "Daddy, come here. Come here."

Moon Pie whinnied and stepped back.

"Remember the horses don't like loud noises," Harvey said, his voice as gentle as it had been with Del when he was a kid.

"Sorry," she whisper-shouted. "Daddy, come here."

Del grinned. "Just a minute, princess."

"Go on," Noah said, handing Uni to him. "I should get to the bakery."

Del grabbed his arm, holding him there. The contact sizzled, and Del bit his lip to keep from saying something he shouldn't. "Thank you. Really. I've got a lot to figure out, but having you here to start with helped a lot."

"Good."

"Mr. Noah, are you leaving?" Clarice asked.

"I am, sweetheart. Your dad is here now, and I need to get

to work."

She frowned. "You promised me a cupcake."

Noah smiled. His acceptance of Clarice was giving Del such strong feelings he could hardly breathe. How could he have forgotten how amazing Noah was?

"I did, but you've got a lot to do here today. I'll talk to your dad, and we'll find a time soon for you to come to my bakery so I can make something very special just for you."

"I want a cupcake now."

"Clarice, Noah doesn't have cupcakes now. We've been keeping him from baking any. He needs time to come up with a special cupcake for you."

Noah nodded. "I do. Special recipes take time."

"Okay. I guess. If you promise."

"I do." Clarice turned back to Moon Pie, and Noah spoke in a low voice. "I think your mom has something special planned for you tomorrow, and I know you need time with her and your dad. The bakery is closed on Sundays, and I don't work Mondays. If Clarice can stand the wait, you could come by Tuesday afternoon. It's not usually busy then, so we can talk."

"That's perfect. We'll be there."

Noah studied him for a moment. "Are you sure you can handle things here?"

"I don't need you to take care of me."

Noah took a step back. "That's not what I meant. I just…"

Shit. He'd snapped at Noah because he was annoyed with himself. "I'm sorry. I didn't mean it like that. I always expected you to take care of everything when we were younger. I don't want to do that to you now."

"You're dealing with a lot right now. I don't mind helping when I can."

Del hated that Noah's voice had lost some of its warmth.

Why did he keep screwing things up? He drew in a shaky breath. “Thank you.”

“You’re welcome.” With a wave to Harvey and Clarice, Noah walked out of the barn.

“Daddy, come see now. Come see.”

“Okay, sweetie.” He could do this. He could smile and pretend he was fine, because he had to be for Clarice. He had to figure out how to live with his parents, and maybe how to… no, he’d better not get his hopes up. Noah was being polite, that was all. He’d stayed because of Clarice, not because he was feeling any of what Del still did.

Del needed to let go of the past and make the best of what he had now. He took Clarice’s outstretched hand and followed her to the next stall in the barn, where a large roan gelding named Bob was munching some hay.

“It’s good to have you back,” Harvey said as Clarice stared at Bob in awe.

“It’s good to see you too.”

They hugged, then Harvey gave Clarice a carrot. “Go ahead. I promise he’s just as gentle as Moon Pie.”

“He’s awesome,” she said, not looking the least bit intimidated.

“Your little girl has quite an affinity for horses,” Harvey said. “I wouldn’t be surprised if she turns out to be an even better rider than you.”

“Do Daddy and I get to race?”

Del nearly choked. “Not for a while, princess. You’ve got to learn how to ride first and—”

“Oh, that’s going to be easy. The horses already love me, so they’ll let me ride them. No problem.”

Del wished he could be as confident about the obstacles he faced. When he looked at Clarice, her joy radiated right to his heart, and he thought maybe he could learn to be.

EIGHT

Noah checked once more to make sure the unicorn cupcakes he'd made for Clarice—one to eat immediately and more to take home and share with her hopefully enthusiastic grandparents—were perfect, or as close to it as he was capable of. They were covered in swirls of pink, purple, and blue icing and sprinkled with edible glitter and silver stars. In the center of each one was a horn made of lemon-flavored swirled stick candy. He hoped she loved them as much as he did.

He'd also made Del his favorite cupcakes, red velvet with cream cheese icing, but he felt sure Clarice would insist Del try one of the unicorn ones. Noah had to admit he wanted to see Del bite into the brightly colored confection. At eighteen, Del would never have touched anything so garish—so gay. But now, Noah bet Del would do whatever it took to make Clarice happy.

Marie pushed through the swinging door into the kitchen. She'd been working at the bakery for several years, and her baking skills were starting to rival Noah's, especially the different breads she made.

“Are those for your man?” she asked, peering over Noah’s shoulder at the cupcakes.

“What?” God knows what his mother had told Marie.

“I heard you have a date this afternoon.”

Noah let himself breathe before responding. “It’s not a date. An old friend is bringing his daughter, because I promised her a cupcake.”

“Friend?” Her eyebrows shot up.

“Yes. Friend.”

“Hmmm.”

“I don’t know what my mom told you, but Del and I never dated in high school, and he left during the summer after graduation. I didn’t see him again until last week.” Noah hated how his voice cracked on the last sentence. He’d totally given himself away.

“Okay, so maybe Lisa is blowing it out of proportion, but…”

Noah sighed. Why couldn’t Marty have been working today instead? He wouldn’t have expected to get the scoop on what was happening. He would have just quietly cleaned up and gone home like he always did, unless he was too busy staring at Del. He wasn’t out to everyone in town, but he’d told Noah he was gay. If Marty flirted with Del, he’d—No. Noah would absolutely not get jealous. That was utterly ridiculous. Del wasn’t his, and Marty could look at whomever he pleased, no matter how much that might make Noah want to strangle him.

I’m fucked.

“So on this not-a-date you’ll be serving these beautiful creations?” Marie asked.

Noah nodded, not trusting himself to speak.

She inspected them more closely. “Wow. Did you make the horns yourself?”

"I did. You want to try one?" Thrilled to be on a much safer topic, he picked up one of the extras and offered it to her.

When she bit into the candy, her face lit up. "It's really good," she said, though she was still chewing. "It's not just pure sugar like I thought it would be. It's lemony and surprisingly refreshing. You've been holding out on us. We need to start a candy line."

"I don't think—"

"I do. You should talk to your mom."

Marie did not look like she was going to let this go. "I don't really think we have time to—"

"Noooo-aaaah." *Speak of the devil.* His mother poked her head into the kitchen. "They just drove up."

Marie patted his shoulder. "Good luck."

Noah sighed. "Mom, can you please just let this be casual?"

"I was only letting you know your date was here."

"It's not a date," he hissed.

"Whatever you say, dear."

"Mom, seriously, I don't want Del to think—"

"I won't say anything to embarrass you; I just want you to be happy."

There was no point in arguing. "Thanks, Mom."

She hugged him, and he kissed her cheek.

"Marie, you can head on out now," he said. "I'll finish cleaning up after they're gone."

"No way. I want to see this famous boy."

"He's not a boy anymore, and oh God, the whole town is going to be like this, aren't they?"

His mom shrugged. "Maybe."

"Fuck."

Noah washed his hands. He wanted to dart into the

restroom and check his hair, but he was sure to be disappointed with his appearance. It was the end of the day, and he was sweaty and covered in flour and who knows what else. His apron rarely caught everything, but at least the t-shirt underneath was cleaner, so he untied the apron, hung it up, and brushed himself off as best he could. Before he could talk himself out of it, he pushed through the swinging door into the front of the bakery.

Del and Clarice were standing at the counter talking to his mom. If Clarice hadn't been there, he'd have been sure he was in a time warp. Yes, Del looked older if Noah paid close attention, but catching him in profile, leaning on the counter on his elbows, he might as well have been eighteen again.

"Noah!" Clarice called.

"Hi, there."

"Where's my cupcake?"

He laughed. She certainly knew what she wanted. "I've got a whole tray of them in the back. Are you ready for me to bring them out?"

"Yes!"

"Clarice," Del said, his tone serious.

"Yes, please and thank you."

"You're welcome." Noah couldn't help but smile. Clarice was going to give Del so much trouble. "I stirred up something special for Clarice, but I also have red velvet if you want it."

"You remembered!" Del's eyes were wide and color rose on his cheeks, making him even more gorgeous.

"Of course I did. Every single birthday, that's the cake you wanted."

Del's color deepened even more. "I just always… I just like it."

"That's Daddy's favorite, but I think it's too red," Clarice announced.

"Well, your cupcakes aren't red at all," Noah assured her.

"Oooh, I want to see. I want to see."

"Ok, wait here."

"Can I get you something to drink?" his mom asked them as he headed back into the kitchen.

Their voices faded as Noah focused on the cupcakes, giving them a final once-over and straightening one of the horns that was leaning.

She's three. She just wants to eat them.

It didn't matter how many times he told himself that, he wanted them to be perfect for her—and for Del. Damn his desire to be what everyone needed. It was never stronger than when he was around Del. He'd hoped that effect had faded, but as soon as he saw Del, it had come back strong as ever, though it didn't feel heavy like it had in high school. Del could take care of himself now. He'd been doing so for years. He had a good job, and he was an amazing dad to Clarice. Still, Noah needed to remember not to let himself get too involved. He'd help Del and Clarice settle in Anticipation. Then they'd get on with their lives, and he'd focus all his energy on the bakery once again.

He picked up the tray and walked back through the swinging door.

Clarice's mouth dropped open and her eyes went wide when she saw the cupcakes. Del's reaction was nearly as dramatic. "Those are amaz—"

"Eeeeeeeeeeeee! They're unicorns. Uni. Uni see them." She held Uni up so he could get a good look. "I want one. I want one. I want one."

"Calm down, princess, and put your bottom on the stool." She was leaning so far over the counter she was in danger of falling. Del laid a hand on her shoulder. Her milk started to tip, but Del caught it in time. He really did have dad instincts. And what that did to Noah—no, he wasn't going to think about it.

Clarice settled down some, but she twisted from side to side until Noah set the tray down.

Noah's mom had already placed a glass of milk, a plate, and a fork in front of her.

"Wow. They're so pretty," Clarice said, her volume only slightly lower this time.

"Thank you."

"Daddy, aren't they pretty?"

For half a second, Del's eyes met Noah's. Noah wasn't sure what he saw there: fear, uncertainty, something intense. "They're beautiful. Noah is the best baker I've ever met."

"I don't really—"

"You are. No arguing."

Arguing with Del had rarely worked, so he focused on Clarice. "Which one would you like?"

Clarice chewed on her bottom lip as she considered. Just like her father.

"That one."

She chose an end one on the row closest to her. Noah picked it up and placed it on her plate. She grabbed it immediately, peeled some of the rainbow paper off and took a huge bite. Colorful icing smeared all around her mouth.

"Mmmmm. So good."

"Chew first," Del admonished.

She squeed as she chewed.

"So you like it, do you?" Del asked.

"It's the best. Daddy, you have to taste. You have to."

Without hesitating, Del bit into the cupcake, which she practically shoved in his face.

His eyes widened as he chewed. After he'd swallowed and licked every bit of icing from his lips—not that Noah was staring or anything—he said, "That is amazing. I thought it would be super sweet, but it's… I don't even know how to describe it other than perfect."

Heat rushed to Noah's face. "Um… Thanks."

"It may be the best cupcake I've ever had, maybe even better than your red velvet."

"It's way better than that," Clarice insisted.

"You've never had one of Noah's red velvet cupcakes."

Clarice shuddered. "They're red."

Del sighed, looking so put upon it made Noah smile.

Clarice looked at her dad and then back at Noah. "Who gets all the other ones?"

"Clarice." Del's tone was sharper now.

Noah shook his head. "It's fine. I'm going to box them up, and you're going to take them home."

"Really?" Her eyes went wide, and she started bouncing again.

"Yes, really, but we might need to give one of them to your dad now. Instead of his *red* one."

She frowned as if considering this and finally said, "All right, but just one."

He looked at Del. "Go ahead, pick one."

"But you… I don't…"

"We put red velvet ones in the case today. I didn't make it just for you, so don't feel bad."

He frowned, considering the cupcake on his plate then the tray of unicorn ones.

"Orrrrr," Noah said, "you could have both."

"I guess I could."

"Do I get two cupcakes?" Clarice asked.

Del narrowed his eyes. "Can you actually eat two cupcakes?"

"I can eat *all* the cupcakes."

"Can you now?"

She nodded vigorously.

"Eat that one first, and we'll see."

"Fine," she said in an exasperated tone. She turned back to her cupcake, grinning as she bit into it and chattering to Uni about how good it was.

Del grabbed a unicorn one and took a bite. Noah tried not to stare at him, but he couldn't help himself.

"What's in these? They really are amazing. They taste a bit citrusy and just… wow."

"The cake recipe is one I often use for wedding cakes, it's an extra moist, white cake with just a touch of lemon, and the icing is the one I put on the dreamsicle cupcakes. It's mildly orange. The horn is lemon stick candy that I formed—"

"You made the horns yourself?"

"I did."

"That's…" He pulled the horn out of the cupcake and studied it. "You twisted it together and everything."

Noah nodded.

Del took a bite of the candy. And grinned as he chewed. "Wow. That's incredible."

Clarice grabbed her horn. "You can eat it?" she asked, looking baffled.

"Yes," Noah said. "It's made out of lemon candy."

She eyed him. "Lemons make you go—" She puckered up her mouth and squinted her eyes.

"What if I called it lemonade candy?"

"I love lemonade!" She bit into hers, and her smile widened. "Mmmmmm."

"See," Marie said. Noah hadn't even noticed her come in from the kitchen. "You need to start making candy to sell."

"Amen," Del said.

"Thank you." Marie held her hand out. "I'm Marie, by the way."

"Oh, sorry," Noah said as Del shook hands with her. "I should have introduced you. This is Del and his daughter Clarice."

"Noah made me unicorns."

"I see that," Marie said. "Those also need to go on the menu."

"Yes!" Noah's mom agreed.

"I don't think—"

"He likes to hide how talented he is, even from me," his mother said. "Like he thinks I didn't pay for culinary school. Like I don't know my boy is a genius in the kitchen."

Noah felt as if his face were on fire.

"Your unicorn cupcakes are going on the menu," his mom declared. "I'm sure Clarice would like to be able to order one whenever she comes in."

"I want to get one every day," Clarice shouted.

"I'm not sure about that," Del said. "But we'll definitely need to have these again."

The door chimed and David and his boyfriend Oliver walked in. Oliver had just moved to Anticipation. He'd said he was there for a few months to see how things went with him and David, but Noah was already certain he was going to stay. The two of them were so obviously head over heels for each other, the way Noah had been with Del that summer after graduation. Could they be like that again?

"Whoa. Are those unicorn cupcakes?" Oliver asked.

"Aren't they bootiful?" Claire yelled.

Oliver grinned at her. "They are."

"Would you like one?" Del asked.

Clarice looked like she was going to protest, but then she sighed and said, "I share with my friends."

Noah bit back a smile, certain she'd heard that phrase many times.

"Thank you." Oliver reached for a cupcake.

"I'm Del and this is my daughter Clarice," Del said.

Dammit, Noah should have introduced them. "I'm sorry. Del, this is David and Oliver. David moved here a few years ago, and he runs a touring company. Oliver's only lived here for a few weeks."

"It's nice to meet you." David held out his hand to Del. They shook, and then David offered his hand to Clarice.

She shook her head. "I'm all sticky."

David grinned. "Thanks for the warning."

"You can have a cupcake too," she said. "I'm a good sharer."

"Thank you, but I'm just here to pick up some muffins I ordered for an early meeting tomorrow," David said.

David watched Oliver as he bit into the unicorn cupcake, warmth in his eyes. Seeing the two of them made Noah long to have what they did, even though he was terrified to hope for it. He glanced at Del and realized he was watching them too. Had he figured out they were a couple?

"Oh my God," Oliver said, mouth still full of cupcake. "I thought your lemon ginger cupcakes were the best, but these are better. You have got to put these on the menu."

Noah's mom slapped him on the shoulder. "See?"

"How did you even come up with this? It's fuc—so amazing."

Noah could tell David was trying not to laugh. It was a running joke that Oliver always seemed to cuss at exactly the wrong moments.

"I was just trying to think of something for Clarice. I didn't really intend—"

"So you'd never made these before?" Del asked, eyes wide.

Noah shook his head. "No."

"You created this recipe just for Clarice?"

Oh shit. He shouldn't have said that, but he wasn't going to be able to get out of it now. If he tried, his Mom would out him. "I did."

Del opened his mouth, closed it, and chewed his lip just like Clarice had done. Noah couldn't make himself look away. "Thank you. That was… I didn't expect anything like that, but I appreciate it."

Clarice glanced up. "Thank you, Mr. Noah."

"You're welcome. I like making up new recipes. I'm glad you like it."

"I do," they both said at the same time, and Noah's chest tightened. He suddenly felt light-headed.

"Here. I'll get your order," Marie said to David.

Oliver cleaned the icing from his mouth and smiled. "It was so nice meeting you." He turned to Clarice. "Thank you for sharing. You're very lucky to get unicorn cupcakes."

Clarice beamed at him.

"Have a good afternoon." Oliver took the rest of his cupcake and headed toward the register where Marie was ringing David up.

Noah's heart hammered as he watched them together. If he stayed there talking to Del, he was going to keep wishing for what Oliver and David had. He couldn't let himself do that. He looked back at Del. "I should probably…"

"Sit down." Del gestured to the chair next to him.

Noah did. As much as he told himself he should, he couldn't walk away.

His mother came over and bent down next to Clarice's chair. "If you're finished, I could show you around the kitchen. You can see where Noah made your cupcakes. We have a mixer that's even bigger than you are."

"Really?" Clarice asked.

Noah's mom nodded.

"Daddy, can I? Please?"

"Here, wipe your hands first." Del pulled a package of wet wipes from the bag he'd set on the floor. Noah could never have imagined Del doing such a thing before he'd left. Yet, it seemed so natural for him. And so… No, Noah was not finding it sexy when Del acted like such a dad. No way.

Clarice took the wipe from him, refusing to let him clean her up. She made a halfhearted effort at doing it herself, then tossed the wipe down and pronounced herself "clean."

Del frowned and glanced at Noah's mom. "Are you sure you don't mind?"

"I would love to get to know Clarice," she said, with a knowing smile that made Noah tense up.

Fortunately, she didn't say anything embarrassing. She just helped Clarice slide down from her chair, took her sticky hand, and led her to the kitchen.

Noah watched them walk through the kitchen door then turned to face Del. The soft way Del was looking at him made him need to swallow before he could speak. "I'm so glad she liked the cupcakes."

"How could she not?"

"I almost called to make sure she liked citrus, but then I decided to risk it." Actually he'd chickened out on calling, afraid he'd end up going to see Del again, because if Del asked, he wasn't sure he could say no.

"Basically, if there's sugar in something, Clarice likes it unless it's—"

"Red." They said the word at the same time and then laughed.

God, Del was gorgeous when he smiled like that.

"So are David and Oliver together?"

"They are."

"And they're out?"

He really wasn't ready to have this conversation with Del. "David just came out as bi a few weeks ago. I'd suspected it, but I don't think many others had. It shocked the hell out of Mrs. Brunnell and Mrs. Lyndon. They had him all lined up to speak at Easter Supper."

Del's eyes widened. "Oh, shit."

"It was quite the scandal, but it died down quickly because everyone loves David. He's just one of those guys who gets along with everyone."

Del nodded. "And Oliver? You said he just moved here."

"That's right. He and David met up at the lodge and… well… things moved really fast and now he's here."

"Wow."

"Yeah."

They sat in silence for a few moments as Del finished his cupcake and sipped on the coffee Noah's mom had served him. Noah knew he should say something, but he wasn't sure what. Finally he settled on, "So how are things with your parents now?"

Del looked down and fiddled with his coffee cup. "Okay, I guess. They… They've been really nice to Clarice but…"

"Not to you?"

"I wouldn't exactly say they haven't been nice, but there's this distance that I can't get past. I apologized, and they told me they love me. I think they forgive me, but things are just… I don't know. Even more awkward than when I was in high school, if that's possible. More polite, but still awkward." Noah started to say something, but Del held up his hand to stop him. "I know I should have seen that coming. I hoped they'd be so happy to find out they had a grandchild they'd kind of forget what I'd done." He shook his head. "God, I'm an idiot."

"Maybe, but all I was going to say was that I'm sorry things are like that."

Del frowned. "Really?"

"Yeah, what good would it do to point out what you already know?"

"You wouldn't have minded doing that five years ago."

Noah bristled, but Del was right. He'd taken care of Del, but he hadn't always been nice about it.

"Shit. I'm sorry," Del said. "I didn't mean to… I just want…"

"What do you want?" Noah's pulse whooshed in his ears. Why had he asked that?

"For this to work."

"This?"

Del looked at him and then away. "Um… Moving back."

"I hope it works for you too." Why did Noah feel disappointed? What had he expected Del to say?

"And… us?"

Go slow, Noah told himself. "I'd like to be friends, to be able to forget our past."

"I don't want to forget it," Del said.

"You don't?"

He shook his head. "No. You were my best friend and my first in so many ways and… Noah, I never forgot any of it. It means too much to me. So much that I was afraid of it, just like I was afraid of this place."

"You hated it here."

"I thought I did, but I missed it. The mountains. The horses. You."

Noah swallowed hard.

"I didn't think I could be happy here or that I could be me here. And five years ago, I couldn't have been. I was too self-conscious, too confused, too… stupid. Maybe I'm still some of those things, but I'm not afraid anymore. If I can raise a little girl, surely I can deal with some people being assholes about who I am."

"Can you really live here and not feel suffocated like you used to?" Noah wasn't convinced Del could.

"I think sometimes it was more about me suffocating myself. I mean, yeah, Anticipation is small, and everybody knows your business."

"They sure as hell do." Noah glanced toward the counter. David and Oliver had left, but Marie was still standing there very carefully counting the stock in the cases as she put it away or packaged it for donating to the food shelter.

She looked up, caught him watching her, and gave him an innocent smile. He didn't really mind her listening in. She was curious for her own sake, but she wasn't a huge gossip. His biggest fear was that she was spying for his mother.

"But I think I'm at a place where I can come to terms with it," Del added.

Was he? And what did that mean for Noah? If Del could truly be happy there, not just grudgingly putting up with Anticipation for Clarice's sake, but truly wanting to stay, then…

Don't get ahead of yourself. He needed to give Del more of a chance to show how he'd changed. There was no question he was more mature, but the old Del was still there. And he wasn't meant to live in a town like Anticipation.

Still…

No.

"So are you going to be working on the ranch or…?"

"I'll still be doing financial planning. My firm takes on contracts from all over the country. We rarely need to be on site to work with clients, so I'll be doing my job from here, taking on fewer contracts of my own until I get settled."

"That's good. Do you think you'll get your own house or stay with your parents?"

"Eventually, I'll need my own place, but I want to give Clarice time to enjoy the ranch, and while I don't really want to live with my parents, I…"

"Need some help?" Noah offered. He could certainly understand that.

Del shook his head. "No. I mean I do, but I can figure that out. I've already started looking at preschools for Clarice. But the ranch is my home. Even when I was gone, when I thought I hated everything about this place, I still associated that land with home." He sighed. "That probably sounds ridiculous."

"No, it doesn't. I get it." Del looked almost as lost as he had that summer after they'd graduated. But this time the memory of their days together was warm and sweet, not bitter the way it had been for years. Had Noah finally forgiven him? He reached out and laid his hand over Del's. "I'm sure your parents will love having Clarice there, and she'll be good for your father, help him get out more."

"I hadn't realized how much he'd aged. The accident was more serious than they ever let on when Mom called to tell me about it. I should've come home then." His eyes shimmered and he turned away, though he gripped Noah's hand tightly, linking their fingers together.

"Your dad is going to be fine. He's already much stronger than he was a few weeks ago. I even saw him at church the Sunday before you got here."

"Really? Mom always had to drag him."

"Well, he likes it more since they changed to our church."

"They did what?" Del looked truly shocked.

"They're Methodists now, because our minister says God loves gay people the same as anyone else."

"But my mother was like the head of everything at church."

Noah chuckled. "She's managed to become quite integral at St. Luke's."

"Wow. I… they didn't tell me." He let go of Noah's hand and took a sip of coffee.

"I think there's a lot the three of you need to talk about."

"Yeah, far more than I knew."

"They love you. They'll come around," Noah said.

"I hope so, but I hurt them. They have every right to be mad at me."

"Yeah, they do." Noah wasn't going to lie to him.

"So do you."

"I was. I… am. But not as much now."

"Really?"

Noah nodded. "You aren't the same man who ran away."

"No, I'm definitely not, though I can still be a selfish idiot sometimes. I'm not going to run again, though. I promise you that."

He held Noah's gaze, and Noah's heart threatened to beat right out of his chest. "O-Okay."

"You believe me?"

Did he? "I want to."

"It's okay. I'll just have to prove it." That confident grin Noah knew so well was back on Del's face. "I'm guessing Oliver and David have dominated town gossip lately, but tell me what else I should know."

Noah explained the rumors about Del's family's neighbor,

Rob Carter, who was also a friend of David's. He'd supposedly been seen at a gay club in Billings and had left with a pair of twinks. He also told Del all about how Ezra, a guy who'd been a few years behind them in school, refused to go to law school like his father and grandfather and was now teaching at the elementary school. On top of that, Ezra was into art and he'd been spending a lot of time with David and Oliver, which meant rumors were flying about his sexuality. Along with all the gossip about gays infiltrating the town, Noah caught Del up on all the weddings and births among their high school classmates.

"Wow, you keep up more than I would've thought," Del said.

Noah snorted. "My mother keeps up and half the town are in and out of here for their morning coffee. You can't help but hear things."

"I guess not."

"Daddy!" Clarice burst through the doorway to the kitchen. "You gotta see what's back there. So many cupcake pans and a mixer this big." She raised her hand as high as it would go. "And a huge oven and—"

Del laughed. "It's really cool, isn't it? I used to go back there with Noah all the time."

"Really? Wow!"

"Your Daddy used to come cook in the kitchen with me and Noah when he was a teenager," Noah's mom said.

"That's right," Del said. "Those are some of my favorite memories."

He glanced at Noah briefly, then looked away, cheeks pink.

Noah's heart stuttered a bit.

"That's awesome. Can I cook with you?" Clarice asked Noah's mom.

His mom glanced at Del, and Del nodded.

"Sure you can. Not today, but I'll talk to your dad, and we'll find a time for you to help. Of course, you could also bake with Noah if you wanted to." His mother gave him a pointed look, which he ignored.

Del pushed his chair back and stood. "Clarice, we need to get going. Grandma is expecting us for dinner soon, and Noah and Ms. Lisa need to clean up so they can go home."

"Can we have cupcakes for dinner?" Clarice asked.

"No, Miss Ella is making fried chicken."

"Yay!" she shouted. "And cupcakes for dessert?"

"Maybe."

"Pleeeease."

"Let's see if Grandma already has dessert planned."

"She'll love the cupcakes."

Del smiled. "I'm sure she will." He turned to Noah. "Clarice is going to ride for the first time tomorrow. Would you like to come watch?"

That wasn't a good idea. Every time they saw each other, Noah fell for him a little harder. "I…"

"Of course he would," Clarice said.

Had he really thought he could refuse? "What time?"

"When are you free?"

"He can be free anytime," Noah's mom said. "He works too hard, and I've been begging him to take some time for himself."

"Let's say one then, right after lunch. That way you'll get your morning baking done, and the bakery won't be too crowded."

"Perfect," his mother answered for him.

He glared at her.

Del grinned. He obviously knew Noah's mom was driving him crazy. "Good, I'll see you then."

"Yeah. See you." Why did his voice have to come out all breathy?

He handed Del the box of cupcakes, and he and Clarice headed out the door. Noah locked it behind them, then turned to face his mother. Marie had cowardly scooted into the back as his mother was arranging a date for him. He would speak to her about her traitorous behavior tomorrow.

"What the hell was that?"

His mother gave him her most charming smile. "That was me keeping you from making a huge mistake."

"He's going to be living here. That was hardly my only chance to see him."

"Clarice adores you. She wants you to see her ride."

Noah had to force himself to unclench his fists. "Are you really going to use a three-year-old against me?"

"She hardly stopped talking about how wonderful you are while she was with me in the kitchen."

That hit him harder than he would have expected. "Really?"

"Yes, you've totally captured her heart."

"And you want me to capture her father's as well."

"I want you to be happy. I want you to get out there and live. I want you to be who you can be."

"I'm a baker. That's what I want to be." A baker. A partner. A dad.

"You could do more than this with your skills."

"What do you want me to do? Go open a bakery in New York?"

His mother gave him the look that said she knew exactly what he was doing. "No. I want you to experiment. Make candy. Make something wild. Start doing more elaborate catering."

"Fill the world with rainbows and glitter?"

"Fuck, yes."

"Oh my God, Mom."

"I'm serious, Noah. You're out, but you're not really being you. That's what I want."

"You think that will work now, because now there's a gay couple in town?"

She shook her head. "There were plenty of gay men here already."

"Not who are out."

"Maybe not, but with some, it's obvious."

"That isn't the same, and you know it."

She nodded. "I do. I'm sorry; I didn't mean to belittle how hard it can be."

He nodded. "Thank you." She looked so worried. "I know you want me to be happy. I'm just… scared." The last word was whispered, but he knew she'd heard, because she pulled him into her arms.

"Don't let fear keep you from something you really want."

"It doesn't matter if I want it and he doesn't."

"The only way you'll find out—"

"Is to try, I know." Noah rolled his eyes. "But last time—"

"Last time you were both eighteen, and everything was new. This is different; I feel it."

He did too, but he wasn't ready to acknowledge that, even to his mother.

"Then we'll see where it goes, but don't—"

"Push. I know," his mom said. "I'll ease off, okay?"

"Okay."

"But—"

He sighed.

"I will make sure you go over there tomorrow and that you look nice."

Oh, hell no. She was not picking out his clothes like he was a kid. "I'm going, but how I look is my decision."

"All right. I can live with that."

NINE

The next day, Noah wore the jeans he'd bought in Casper that showed his ass to perfection and a purple button-down—not at all because one time, after someone had made fun of a sweater he owned in high school, Del had told him he looked amazing in purple. A little before one, Noah attempted to sneak out the back door of the bakery. But apparently his mother really did have eyes in the back of her head. She whirled around from where she was mixing cookie dough before he could make his escape.

"I boxed up some muffins for you to take." She picked up a box and held it out to him then set it back down when she saw he already had a box in his hands. "Did you already get some?"

"No, but I've got to run." He pushed the door open.

"Noah, what's in that box?"

He sighed. There was no way he was getting out of there without telling her. "It's a pie."

Her eyes went wide. "A pie?"

"Yes. You know. Round pastry filled with fruit."

"You never make pies for people unless…"

"Don't make a big deal out of it. I just thought Clarice—"

"You have a whole hierarchy of baked goods and pie is at the top."

Why had he ever explained his gifting rules to his mom? She was right though, pie said you cared for someone—loved someone. And just like he'd known brownies were the right thing to take when he'd picked Del up at the airport, he knew that cake was appropriate for today's visit. A friend, wanting to impress but not wanting more than friendship, brought cake. And yet, he'd made a pie. This was escalating much too fast.

"It's too much, isn't it?" he asked his mom.

"Does Del know your system for deciding who gets what kind of baked good?"

"Not exactly." Most of that had solidified in Noah's mind after culinary school. "But he does know I don't make pies for just anyone, or at least he used to. Maybe he doesn't remember." Yeah. He'd hold on to that thought.

His mother's expression said he was fooling himself.

"What kind of pie did you make?"

"Blueberry."

She frowned.

"Yes, I remember that cherry is his favorite, but it's red."

She laughed. "Of course it is. And you want Clarice to eat it too."

"Right. I'm going now, Mom."

"Go." She waved him away. "Have fun."

He pulled the door shut behind him and prayed he hadn't gone too far with the pie.

Del paced the length of the front porch. It was cold

as hell, but he didn't care. He couldn't stand being cooped up inside any longer. And that made no sense at all after having lived in an apartment not much larger than the suite of rooms he had here. But his parents were making him feel smothered —okay, his mom was. His dad was spending most of his time telling her to just let him be. No wonder his dad was willing to resort to anything to get out of the house, even attending a church he supposedly didn't like.

The sound of a vehicle coming up the drive interrupted his thoughts.

Please be Noah. Please be Noah.

He'd almost texted Noah to make sure he was still coming, but that was too desperate, too demanding, too everything he'd been before.

A truck rounded the corner, and Del breathed a sigh of relief. It was Noah. Del should have known he'd never let Clarice down, at least not without calling. It didn't mean Noah was eager to see him, but at least he was here. Noah's mother sure seemed eager for them to spend more time together. Lisa had always been a matchmaker, and if she were on his side, that was a step in the right direction.

Noah waved to him as he pulled to a stop. When he stepped out, he circled to the passenger side and—was that a bakery box he was pulling out? It sure looked like it. Even before Noah had gone to culinary school, back when he was just helping his mom at the bakery, he'd almost always brought food whenever he'd come over.

"What have you got there?" Del called.

"Before I reveal that, you have to tell me what the hell you're doing on the porch in this weather. I would've figured you'd gone too soft for this."

Del snorted. "Hardly. Don't you know Chicago is the Windy City? Winter there is no joke."

Noah just shrugged.

"I needed to get away. I can't think in there." He used his thumb to gesture over his shoulder to the house.

"That could prove problematic if you're going to live here."

Del sighed. "It'll get better. I hope it will, at least."

"Maybe this will help for now," Noah said, holding out the box.

Del peered through the clear top. "That's a pie."

"Very observant."

"But you… But pie is…"

"The ultimate thing to bake for someone."

It was more than that to Noah. It was something you baked for someone you loved, or at least that's what he'd said years ago. It didn't have to be romantic love. He'd baked one for a teacher who had been a mentor to him. But pie meant he loved Del to some extent. Even if it was the love of a friend, that meant there was hope for them.

"What flavor?" It had a lattice top like cherry, but the color was wrong.

"It's blueberry. Cherry is red, so…"

Del couldn't have been more touched that Noah had accepted Clarice's aversion to red foods. While most people just laughed it off, Noah hadn't even teased her about it.

"Clarice will be thrilled; she loves blueberries."

"I'm glad. I made the top that way because you were always so impressed by it." Noah seemed to realize how his words could be interpreted and paused.

"Thank you." Del laid a hand on his arm, and Noah's eyes widened just a fraction. Then he coughed and looked away.

"You're welcome."

"I'll take it inside and get Clarice."

"Is she doing okay?"

"Better than me. Of course, my mom is showering her with attention."

"That's good, right?" Noah asked.

"Yes, I wanted Clarice to love them and for them to accept her, and they have. I just—"

"Wish they'd accept you?"

He shook his head. "I wish I felt sure they'd forgiven me."

"You were hoping they'd kill the fatted calf?"

Del scowled. "Hey!"

"You can't expect it to happen instantaneously."

"I know. I don't think it's going to be easy. Not anymore. Not after…"

Noah laid his hand on Del's shoulder. It was warm and reassuring. It had been too long since he'd had someone who could comfort him through touch. Since before Amy died.

"I know. I'm sorry," Noah said.

Del nodded without turning around. Then Noah dropped his hand, and they walked inside.

"Noah," Del's mom exclaimed. "How nice to see you again."

Del got the feeling she was wondering if Noah was going to be around all the time like he had been in high school.

"He brought a pie," Del said.

"Oh, how lovely." His mother took the box from him. "We can have it after dinner."

"Actually, I was going to have some after Clarice's ride."

"Yes! Yes! Yes!" Clarice said, racing into the room. "I love pie!"

His mother sighed and pursed her lips. Nothing had changed there. She hated to be contradicted, and she rarely allowed spontaneous treats.

Clarice ran up and hugged Noah's legs. "You made me a pie?"

"I made it for you and your dad."

"I can be a sharer," she said as she raced across the room to Del. "Can I ride now? Noah's here. You said when he was here that we'd do riding."

"Just a second, sweetheart." Del turned to his mom. "We're going to take Clarice out to the barn. Do you want to join us?"

She looked pained for a moment, like she wasn't sure how to answer.

"It's okay if you have other plans."

"I have a meeting in town. I wish you'd told me yesterday. I might have been able to rearrange my schedule."

He should have, and if Noah hadn't been coming he probably would have, but while he felt obligated to invite her, he really wanted this time with Noah and Clarice.

"I have a feeling she'll be spending a lot of time with the horses, so you can see her ride some other time." Or not. His mother was loving doing things with Clarice like letting her try on jewelry or even dying Easter eggs—while wearing protective gloves, of course. But for a woman who owned a ranch, she spent very little time in the barn. His dad had always been part of the day-to-day operations, but his mother was content to let the ranch make money and never actually think about all those big, smelly animals. To be fair, she'd been nothing but encouraging about Clarice's love of horses. Probably because she thought it would fade. For all Del knew, it would, or the reality wouldn't live up to the fantasy. But he was going to let Clarice go full tilt as long as it lasted. She deserved that.

"What about Dad? Is he around?"

"He's gone out with Harvey to look at some of the cattle."

"But I thought—"

"They're taking the four wheelers, and your father insists he's done with sitting inside." She huffed. "I tried, but I couldn't do a thing to stop him."

"Maybe he'll rest once he gets in," Del said.

"Maybe." She shooed them toward the door. "You run along now."

Clarice was holding on to the doorknob and bouncing. "Let's go. Let's go."

He laughed. "All right. We're coming."

The three of them made their way along the shoveled path, but Clarice occasionally stepped off into the deep snow, seeming to find that hilarious. At least she was wearing snow boots. She didn't have riding boots yet. She was only going to be walked on a lead rope, so she'd be fine for now.

When they stepped into the barn, Del was immediately too warm. How high did they have the heat cranked? Or was it just that Noah was right there by his side? He couldn't stop being nervous every time they were together, because no matter how much he scolded himself for it, he wanted everything he'd given up when he ran away.

"Moony!" Clarice squealed when she saw the pony.

"Clarice." She skidded to a stop. She knew the tone Del had used. "What did I say about running in a barn?"

"Um… I could get hurt."

"That's right. You could get hurt, and it also scares the horses."

"You hear that, Uni," Clarice said to her companion. "You better walk so horses aren't scared."

Del looked over at Noah, who was clearly trying not to laugh. He wanted to take Noah's hand, but this wasn't the time for him to explain how he felt.

They took their time getting Moon Pie brushed and tacked

up despite Clarice's impatience and pestering. Del had known she'd want to ride the moment she stepped into the barn, but he believed it was important for her to know how to care for horses if she was going to ride them.

Clarice handed Uni to Noah before Del helped her mount. Then he took the lead rope, and they started slowly out of the barn.

"I'm riding. I'm riding," Clarice shouted.

"Remember Moon Pie likes quiet voices," Noah said, no hint of scolding, just a simple statement.

"Right," she whisper-yelled. "I forgetted."

Del noticed that Noah was cradling Uni carefully like he had the other day. The sight melted Del's heart. Noah was an even better man than Del had remembered.

Clarice was so in awe of her experience she hardly spoke as they walked down the path toward one of the pastures.

When Del decided it was time to end the ride while Clarice was still happy rather than melting down after getting tired, he said, "Do you want to learn how to dismount?"

"No." She shook her head. "I want to stay on forever."

"I bet you do, but Moon Pie is tired."

"No she's not. She wants to ride more. She likes it."

"She does like it, but she's ready for a treat and some rest time."

"No!"

"Uni wants to hear all about your ride," Noah said. "But he can't until Moon Pie is taken care of."

Noah was so good with Clarice. Del was officially in love.

Clarice frowned at Del. "I don't want to stop."

"We can have pie before your nap."

Her eyes lit up. "Pie?"

"Noah's pie that he made especially for us."

"Fine. I'll tell Uni all about it while I eat pie."

"Perfect. Now hold on here." He pointed to the pommel. "And bring your foot over Moon Pie's back."

She did as he said.

"Good. You're a natural." He helped her slide off the horse, then handed her the lead rope. "You can walk her back to the barn."

Her eyes went wide. "Really?"

"Yes. I'll be right behind you. Don't go inside without me or Noah."

Noah opened the barn door when Clarice reached it, and Del picked up his pace so he could be by her side. "Take her right to her stall, okay?"

"Okay!" Clarice said.

As Clarice headed into the barn, Del let his hand brush Noah's arm. "Thank you."

"You're welcome." Noah looked up, meeting Del's gaze, and a shiver ran along Del's spine. There were still feelings between them. No way was he imagining it.

TEN

"That pie was amazing," Del said as they walked along the plowed path.

Noah's cheeks were pink, and Del wondered if it was only from the cold. "Thanks."

Del had asked Noah to take a walk with him after they'd finished their snack, and Clarice had reluctantly agreed to some "quiet" time in her room, saying she didn't need a nap, but she supposed she could read to Uni. He almost hated to miss that, because listening to her make up elaborate stories based on the pictures in books was one of his favorite things. He bet Noah would love it too. He needed some time alone with Noah, though.

The snow was packed beneath their feet, making it easy to walk. Del didn't mind the cold, because he and Noah were finally on their own, the air was fresh and clean, and the mountains were beckoning him like they had when he was a kid.

Del scanned the path in front of them. "You think we can get all the way up to our favorite spot?"

Noah scrunched up his nose, seeming to consider the

question. "The snow's pretty deep, but maybe. You really want to go up there?"

"I do. I missed it, and I… I want to see it again with you."

Noah glanced away, something unreadable in his eyes. Del prayed he wasn't fucking things up.

"You do?"

"Yeah."

"Why?"

Del sighed. "Because it was ours and…"

"You went up there alone too. You said it was one of the only places you were really able to think."

"I obviously didn't think too clearly, or I wouldn't have run."

"Did you go up there that day? When you decided to leave?"

He nodded. "Yeah, I couldn't sleep, so I went up there to see the sunrise. I almost called you to see if you wanted to join me, but then I got scared and overwhelmed. I kept thinking how you'd want me to stay here."

"I didn't—"

"Shh." He placed a finger against Noah's lips, then pulled back quickly. The soft skin was far too seductive. "I'm not blaming you. That was all me, what was in my head. I started thinking how I couldn't do it, couldn't be me here or maybe anywhere. I wished I could change who I was. Then I hated myself for thinking that, because you were the best thing that has ever happened to me." There, he'd said it.

Noah stared at him, not saying a word. At least he wasn't running away.

After a few moments, Noah said, "I never wanted to change you."

Del raised his brows.

"All right. Maybe I did want you to be a little less self-centered, a little more willing to—"

"Man up and quit expecting you to take care of me?"

Noah winced. "I sound like an ass."

"No, you were right."

"I never wanted you to be someone else, someone who would love living here."

Neither of them said anything for a while. Then Noah broke the silence. "I think I did resent that you couldn't try, even though I refused to try living in a big city. Shit. I'm sorry."

"You had a reason to stay in Anticipation."

"Not a good one, according to my mom."

"But you stayed for her."

"She says she'd be fine without me, and that I should do what I want, not what I think she wants me to do."

Del laughed. "Yeah, I can see her saying that."

"For what it's worth, I really did understand why you had to leave," Noah said.

Del had to swallow before he could speak. Even then his voice shook. "I'm so sorry I hurt you."

"You still want to make the climb?" Noah asked, thankfully ignoring that Del sounded close to tears.

Del glanced back toward the house. It would be a hard climb, but he didn't want to turn back. "Yeah."

"Good. I've missed our spot too."

"You haven't been up there since I left?" Del asked, not sure why that shocked him so much.

"No. At first I didn't want to be reminded of you, of what we'd shared. By the time I was okay with the memories, it felt intrusive. It was hard enough for your parents, hardly ever hearing from you. They didn't need the boy who ran you off climbing around on their land."

"They didn't really think that about you, did they?"

"Your mom never said it outright, and you know how quiet your dad is, but it was clear they didn't see me as blameless."

"I'll talk to them, make them understand."

"I don't need you to do that, and there's a bit of truth in it anyway, isn't there? If we'd never been together, you wouldn't have run."

Del wasn't sure what to say to that. It was true, and yet it was such a simplified version of the truth that it almost wasn't.

As they started to climb the hill toward the secluded spot where they'd spent so much time together in high school, Del thought about how they'd had their first kiss there. Then later that night he'd snuck out, climbed through Noah's window, and they'd shared their first time. That had led to him sneaking out again and again, until he'd finally asked for what he really wanted, what he'd always fantasized about, and he'd loved it so much, he'd run.

Looking back now, he wondered if Noah's mother had known when he was there. Heat filled his face as he realized how likely it was that she had. He doubted they'd been as discreet as they meant to be.

When they reached the top of the hill and found the stand of trees that protected a small clearing, Del sucked in his breath. It was beautiful with the trees covered in snow. He and Noah had rarely come up here in the winter. Most of their time together was spent looking out at the green hills in summer.

Del turned to look at Noah, and his breath caught when he saw the longing in Noah's eyes.

"I… I want…"

Del nodded. "Yeah, me too."

Noah stepped closer then, but Del didn't touch him. He needed Noah to make the first move. Del had no right to expect anything from him. He'd run. He'd ignored Noah when he'd texted and then called again and again. He'd been an asshole and—

Noah cupped his face. "I think I've lost my mind to consider this."

"Yeah, probably."

Noah leaned closer, his lips almost touching Del's. Del hardly dared breathe. Noah licked Del's lower lip and Del whispered, "Please."

"God help me." Noah kissed Del then, not a slow, gentle touching of lips, but a kiss that was full of all the pent-up passion from those five years apart. A kiss full of anger and fear. Del gave back all of that and more.

Noah's thumb caressed Del's cheek, a soft counterpoint to the biting and tongue-thrusting of the kiss.

Del gripped Noah's waist, yanking them closer, wishing they weren't in layers of clothes. He needed to feel Noah, to touch his skin. He slid his tongue along Noah's, groaning into his mouth. God, he'd needed this warmth. Would they get frostbite if they ripped off their clothes and fucked right there in the snow?

Noah pulled back, and Del tried to hold on to him, using his body to ask for more, because he couldn't form words. But Noah shook his head, and Del had to let him go. If he pushed too hard, he'd never convince Noah to try again with him.

Noah didn't say anything. He just stared at Del, breath ragged.

Del licked his lips and swallowed, willing his dick to calm down. No matter how much it wanted Noah, he wasn't actually going to risk freezing it off.

"That was… I… Are you okay?" Wow. He was eloquent.

Noah nodded slowly. "I am. And yeah. That was amazing."

"Do you… um?"

Noah shook his head. "It's way too cold."

Holy shit. He'd been thinking it too. "Should we head back or…"

Noah shook his head. "I'm not ready to go back. I want to hold on to this a little longer."

"Being up here?"

"Being with you, pretending things are like they were years ago when there was a world of possibility in front of us."

"There still is."

Noah frowned. "What?"

"There's still a world of possibility. We could do anything."

Noah laughed, and Del hated how bitter he sounded. "You sound like my mom. She's always telling me I should try new things, seek out bigger opportunities."

"Why haven't you? I know you didn't want what I did: big city, fancy apartment, high-powered job. But you are an incredible baker, and you could—"

"I'm not going to abandon my mom. She doesn't have anyone else here. I mean she has friends and all, but no other family, and I just…" He ran a hand over his hair as if he'd forgotten he was wearing a hat. Del caught his beanie when it fell and held it out to him.

"Shit. I'm a mess," Noah said. "Maybe we should go."

Del caught his arm. "Talk to me. God knows you had to listen to me go on and on all the damn time when we were in high school. The least I can do is be here for you now."

"All right. I could've gotten a job somewhere bigger—

Billings at least—but I love these mountains and this little town, problematic as it can be. I know my mom says she's fine, and she is. But what if… something happened, and I was far away, and no one was there?"

There were so many things Del could say: no one could know what would happen, Noah's mom wanted the best for him, Noah deserved to have something for himself. Instead, he simply took Noah's hand and squeezed it. With a gentle tug, he turned them so they were both looking out over the pastures.

"Being up here again, I understand why you love this place so much. But there's more you could do without leaving Anticipation. There are so many tourists here these days, you could cater more to them, make candies, team up with some bed and breakfasts or Airbnb hosts."

"We do catering," Noah said.

"You do weddings for locals. I'm talking far more than that."

"I'm just not sure—"

"Noah, what are you afraid of?"

Noah started to say something, then shook his head. "That's not—I don't want to talk about this anymore, okay?"

"Okay." Del wanted to push, and he was known for goading people until they got angry—he'd done it to his parents all the time—but he forced himself to hold back.

"So what about you?" Noah asked. "What about your talent?"

"My talent for what, getting in trouble? Pissing people off? Being a self-centered jerk?"

Noah scowled at him. "Is that how Clarice sees you?"

Damn Noah and his ability to push through Del's barriers. Why was he putting up a front with Noah anyway? He'd told himself he'd be open and honest, but it hurt even more than he expected for Noah to see him raw and exposed.

"No," Del choked the word out.

"It's not how I see you either, not even after you ran."

Del pressed his hand against his eyes, fighting the urge to cry. He'd been sure Noah hated him. That was part of why he never called. "I don't deserve that."

"A second chance? I thought that was what you wanted?"

"I do want it, but—"

"Then you need to believe you deserve it if you want me to."

"And you need to stop being afraid of success."

"I'm not—" He looked away, holding himself rigid.

"Noah, I've known you a long time."

"No." His voice was quiet, almost too low for Del to hear him. "You knew me a long time ago."

Del's breath whooshed out as the pain of Noah's words made him want to double over. "That. Right there. That's what I deserve."

"Shit."

"No, it's okay for you to be angry. It's okay for you to need help and advice or—"

"Stop!"

Del froze.

"Don't be so fucking nice. It's not… you."

Del had no idea what to say to that. Noah was right, though. Nice wasn't something he'd ever been known for, at least not until Clarice had come to live with him.

"We should go." He turned toward the path, but Noah grabbed his arms and spun him back around.

"This was never going to be easy."

"Me coming back here?"

"Us."

"It used to feel easy."

"It used to feel easy, because I let it," Noah said. "I protected you."

"So it was easy for me, because I'm an asshole?" Del asked.

Noah ignored him. "I wanted you from the day we met."

"Why?" The word came out as a sob. Del wanted to sink into the ground.

"I have no idea. I just did."

"You could have told me sooner."

Noah rolled his eyes. "Like I was going to tell the rich, cool rancher's son that I'm gay, that I jerk off thinking about him, that I make him pie because I want him to see me. The real me."

"I did see you. I wanted to be with you more than anyone else."

Noah nodded, his anger seeming to dissipate. "I know, and I thought about risking it long before you said anything."

"Being with you felt so right. So much better than anything else."

"Yeah, it did, but if we'd let it be more there would've been no way to make that simple. And I didn't think… I didn't think you'd be willing to do complicated."

Del brushed tears from his cheeks. "I'm sorry. I really am."

"You didn't even answer a single text."

Del nodded. "I couldn't let myself, because if I did, I'd run right back to you, and then I would've made us both miserable."

"You did that anyway by staying away." This time Noah was the one to turn away and start for the path.

"Noah?"

He didn't turn around.

"Please."

He stopped, and Del hurried as fast as he could in the snow.

"Please give me a chance. Even if I don't deserve it, even if you hate me right now."

"I never hated you." The words burst from him, harsh and angry, as if he wished he had.

"Not even when I first left?"

"Maybe for just a little bit, but I lo—I wanted you too."

"I loved you, and it terrified me."

Noah looked up at him, eyes wide. "You what?"

"I loved you, and oh fuck, I shouldn't have said that."

"Del, I… I don't…"

He sighed. He'd fucked up again. "I didn't want you to think I just ran and forgot you. I never stopped thinking about you, but I didn't mean to just blurt that out. I was supposed to take this slow. I was supposed to let us be friends again and not put any pressure on you. I'd made a plan and everything. Shit!" He sounded like a lunatic.

But Noah was smiling. "Del, when did your plans ever work?"

He laughed then when he would've thought that impossible. "Never."

"And when did you ever hold back when you wanted to say something?"

Del inhaled slowly. "That night. When you… when we…"

"When I tied you up and spanked you?"

"You make it sound so—"

Noah raised his brows.

"It was… Fuck, it was special."

"I know." Noah's voice was low and rough, and tears burned behind Del's eyes.

"So that night… I wanted to tell you how I felt back then."

"So instead you slipped out when I was asleep, left town, and never spoke to me again."

"Um… yeah."

"So about par for the course for your planning."

"Noah!"

He smiled. "I'm going to give you another chance."

"You are?"

Noah nodded. "Don't you see that I already am? I'm here, aren't I?"

"I thought you just came because Clarice… and your mom and…"

"I actually can say no to my mom."

Del stared at him.

"On occasion. Okay, I've said no a few times."

Del laughed. "She's pretty scary when she's determined."

"She is, but I wouldn't be here if I wasn't willing to see where things could go with us, because me hanging around with you, even for Clarice's sake, would be cruel otherwise."

"I was afraid you were just being friendly."

"Seriously, Del? I think it was clear from the moment we saw each other at the airport that we can't just be friends."

"Okay, fair point. So what are we?"

Noah studied him for a moment. "I'm not ready to decide that yet."

"Friends with benefits?" He gave Noah a coy look.

"Ah. There's the Del I remember."

"I'm joking."

"Are you?" Noah asked.

Was he serious? Did he want more? "Wait. Are you not?"

"I don't know. I can't decide quite how stupid that would be."

"I want you, but if you don't feel the same way, I'm not some horny eighteen-year-old who's going to climb in your window."

Noah grinned. "I loved that, actually. And I know you're not the same man who left here, or you wouldn't be raising Clarice on your own."

"I'd like to think I was never such an asshole that I'd abandon a little girl who didn't have any other family."

"Oh God, no. I didn't mean that. You were full of yourself like most teenagers, but you were never cruel."

"I used you," he confessed.

"I was obsessed with you and stupid."

"That doesn't make it okay."

"No, it doesn't, but we're older now and more confident."

"Maybe. Sometimes, especially with Clarice, I have no idea what I'm doing."

"I always wondered what it would take to stop you from being arrogant and demanding. I guess now I know."

How did he not know? That's why he'd wanted Noah to make him submit, to punish him. He craved Noah stripping away his arrogance, making him surrender, making him do whatever Noah wanted. He wouldn't have to pretend to know what to do then.

"What's that look for?" Noah asked.

"What look?"

"The one that says you're thinking something dirty."

"Maybe I am."

"Are you going to share?"

"Do you want me to?"

Noah gave Del a slow once-over, and Del grew desperate to kiss him again.

"Not now. Not here."

"Probably sensible." They really did need to wait until they were indoors and somewhere private.

"Okay."

They held hands as they walked back down the hill, but once they were in sight of the house, Noah let go, and Del didn't protest.

"I'm not ready for questions about us," Noah said. "Of course, I'm sure we're the number one gossip topic for at least half the town, but let's not give them a reason to ask directly, not yet anyway."

Del knew Noah was right, even if he wanted to tell everyone Noah was his.

"Of course it won't help that my mom was practically throwing me at you."

Del smiled. "I didn't mind."

Noah laughed. "I kind of guessed that."

"You really think we've made that big of a stir already?"

Noah sighed. "Probably bigger than you'd like to think. There was, as I'm sure you know, a lot of speculation about why you ran. And while your parents never said anything against me, the idea that I'd run you off was one of the top theories."

Del stopped walking. "Wait. Are you serious?"

"Yeah. Me pressuring you to come out supposedly scared you off."

"Oh God, Noah, I didn't know, and you never pressured me."

Noah frowned. "I did. A bit."

"No, you just—"

Noah cut him off. "I left for culinary school not long after you ran, so it was okay."

"No, nothing about that is okay."

"Fine. It wasn't, but I survived."

"Why didn't someone tell me?"

"I did, but you ignored my message."

He'd deleted all of Noah's voicemails, and most of his texts had just said "call me."

"I am a horrible person."

Noah gave him a soft smile. "You were scared. And young. And a little horrible."

"Oh God. I don't know how I'll ever make up for what I did."

"Wanting to is a good start."

They were walking again and approaching the house much too quickly. As hard as their conversation had been, Del wasn't ready for this time alone with Noah to end. Maybe Clarice would fall asleep and—There she was, waving frantically from the front window. Did his mother know she'd snuck into the formal living room?

"So much for quiet time," Del said.

Noah laughed. "You really do have your hands full."

"I do." And it would be great to have a partner to share it with.

Whoa. He was getting too far ahead of himself, but in the few days he'd been home, he'd realized he really did want that—the house and white picket fence, or pasture fence rather, kids, and a man to share it with. Correction. Noah to share it with.

"Are you okay?"

"Yeah. Thank you for being here."

"You're welcome. I want you to call me if you need me, okay?"

"I will. Are you going now?"

"I think I should. We both need some time to process all this."

Del nodded. Noah was probably right, but part of him

wanted Noah to stay, even though he knew he couldn't use him as a buffer. He had to face the reality of making things right with his family all on his own.

"So I'll see you soon?" Noah asked.

"Yes. I'll text you tomorrow."

Del wanted to kiss him goodbye, but he didn't. He just watched Noah as he walked to his truck. Then he rushed inside before Clarice could decide to join him in the snow.

ELEVEN

Noah usually loved his days off, possibly even more so because he worked on Saturdays and then had Sunday and Monday to himself. He loved being able to take care of errands on Mondays when the town was much quieter. But Del had been in town for over two weeks now, and they still hadn't managed to spend any more time alone. After seeing Del at church with his parents and Clarice, who loudly questioned everything about the service to the amusement of everyone around her, Noah had spent the rest of the day thinking about Del and wondering what he was doing. And now on Monday morning he was still considering calling Del or dropping by the ranch with something he'd baked. Noah's mom always laughed that he still baked on his days off, but even after years of doing it professionally it was what he loved most.

Maybe he could make a coffee cake and take it to Del before he did his weekly grocery shopping. He glanced at the time. It was only eight. Waking up as early as he did often made the day seem like it was passing slowly. Still, he bet Del had eaten breakfast already. The day started early on a ranch, not quite as early as at a bakery, but much earlier than eight. And he doubted Clarice would want to miss a minute of her time with the horses, especially since Del had said she might be starting preschool this week.

Not that coffee cake couldn't be enjoyed for second breakfast or morning snack, but… ugh, he needed to stop obsessing. He should just call Del and say he wanted to see him. Just him. Maybe naked. In bed.

Or he could just make a coffee cake and eat it himself while he agonized some more. He sighed, put down the book he hadn't really been reading, and walked to the kitchen.

He pulled down a notebook where he'd collected recipes people had given him and his mom. He flipped through it until he found what he was looking for: his great-aunt Linda's sour cream coffee cake. It was a basic recipe, but it never failed to please.

He quickly lost himself in the soothing rhythm of stirring up the simple cake and making the streusel topping.

A few minutes later, he slipped it in the oven, set a timer, and returned to the couch. He still didn't think he could focus on reading, so he reached for the remote, but it wasn't where he thought he'd left it. He bent down to look under the couch, and nearly toppled over when the doorbell rang, surprising the hell out of him.

"Coming," he called as he hurried across the room. It was probably someone from the bakery. About a year ago, after many requests to serve lunch, they'd added a few sandwiches and a hot item of the day to their menu. His mom usually sent food over for him on his day off.

He was wrong. It was Del.

"Oh. I thought you were…" He suddenly realized he'd answered the door wearing a torn t-shirt, pajama bottoms he'd had since high school, and an apron with a rainbow on it.

Del frowned. "I can go if—"

"No!"

"No?"

"Come in. I just… I should change."

Del looked him up and down and smiled. "I like it."

Noah's face grew even warmer. "Were you just stopping by, or did you need something?"

Del chewed on his lip. Then he looked up, and their gazes met. The heat in Del's eyes had Noah mesmerized.

"You," Del said.

"What?"

"You are what I need."

"Oh fuck."

Del smiled. And Noah was suddenly glad he was in pj bottoms, because if he had put on jeans, they would have gotten way too tight.

He stepped back so Del could enter. Then he shut the door behind him.

"Do you have any plans this morning?" Del asked.

"Um… no. I was… um… making a coffee cake."

"How long does it need to cook?"

"Maybe half an hour or so. Where's Clarice?"

"Preschool."

Noah's breath caught. "So you're on your own?"

"Until one."

Wow, that was like four hours. Plenty of time to get Del naked and take what he wanted, maybe more than once. He knew it was foolish, he knew he was likely to get hurt, probably even worse than he had when Del left, but he'd wanted Del ever since he'd seen him at the airport. There was no way in hell he could walk away from the need in Del's eyes.

"Were you expecting someone?" Del asked.

"What? Huh?"

"You seemed surprised that it was me at the door," Del said. "I thought maybe you were expecting someone else."

"Oh, no, not really. Sometimes my mom sends lunch over, but usually not this early. If I don't answer the door, they'll just leave it on the porch."

"But your car is here."

"They'll assume I'm in the shower or on a walk or something. I don't really care."

All he could think about was Del and how amazing he looked standing there. He grabbed the lapels of Del's coat and hauled him in for a kiss. Del's arms went around him, and they devoured each other until Noah thought he might pass out from the lack of air.

When they finally pulled apart, they stared at each other, both panting.

"Five fucking years, Del. I shouldn't still want you this badly."

"I know. But you do, so let me remind you why." Del dropped to his knees, almost toppling over as he struggled to get out of his coat.

Noah untied his apron, pulled it off, and tossed it toward the kitchen. He wondered if he should check on the cake, but after Del pushed Noah's shirt up and ran his tongue along the edge of Noah's waistband, he decided he didn't care what happened to the cake.

He looked down, and the sight of Del Crane on his knees made him dizzy. "Del, do you still… Do you want me in control?"

"Yes. So much. Yes." He traced a finger along Noah's straining erection, making him gasp.

"More," Noah demanded.

"I want to give you so much more." Del gripped Noah's hips and leaned his forehead against Noah's abdomen.

"Oh, God, Del. You don't have to do this."

"I want to. I want this more than I've ever wanted anything."

"More than you wanted it that last night before you left?"

Del groaned, the sound so full of anguish it made Noah's chest ache.

"I won't leave this time," he said, his voice so low Noah barely heard him.

"O-Okay." Noah petted him, running his hands over Del's hair. He wanted this so badly, but he also wanted it to be less complicated.

Del looked up at him, and he must have felt reassured by what he saw on Noah's face, because he hooked his fingers in the waist of Noah's pants. "I need to see you."

Noah lifted the hem of his t-shirt, drew it over his head, and threw it on top of his apron.

"Mmm," Del groaned. "Just as hot as ever."

"Del, you don't have to—"

"Hush." He nipped at Noah's stomach, making him yelp. "You're fucking gorgeous."

Del pushed Noah's pajamas down, and his eyes went wide. "Wow, you're not wearing anything under there."

"It's my day off. Why would I? I just—" Del stroked his cock, and his words evaporated.

"I've dreamed about this," Del whispered, his mouth so close to Noah's cock that Noah could feel his warm breath.

"My cock?"

"Sucking you off."

Noah's knees threatened to buckle. "Seriously?"

"Yes. I've jerked off to the thought of it so many times, that and you fucking me, opening me up, making me beg."

This wasn't real. It couldn't be, and he wasn't sure he could fall back into the vibe they'd had so many years ago, when despite what anyone who knew them would think, he'd been the dominant one in the relationship. Of course, he'd topped guys since then, but he'd never been in control the way he had with Del. Sure, he'd fumbled his way through it, having no idea what he was doing, but it had felt so right and now… "Have you done this with anyone else?"

"Fucked?

Noah shook his head. He didn't think Del had been celibate all these years, but he didn't want to think about his partners. "No, been… you know… dominated."

Del shook his head. "Never. I don't know if I could trust anyone but you."

Dear God, the things those words did to Noah. Before he could think of what else to say, Del licked the underside of his cock, and suddenly that was all Noah could think about.

"Tell me what to do," Del whispered.

Noah took a deep breath. He could do this.

"I want to know what you like best." Del dipped his tongue into Noah's slit, preventing Noah from putting words together in any sensible order. "You have been with men since we fucked, right?" Del kept his voice low and sultry. Noah could easily get lost in the sound.

"I… um… yes. I slept with a lot of men in culinary school. Well, not a *lot*, but several and I… I like to be in control. I like what we had."

"You like to drive into a guy's ass, to give it to him hard, the way you want to?"

"Fuck, Del." He had no idea Del had such a filthy mouth.

"You like when I talk dirty?"

"Yes."

Del worked Noah's cock with his hand as he grinned at

him, looking more relaxed than he'd been since he'd returned. Had getting on his knees really done that for him?

Noah hadn't ever thought he was good at talking. He was better at doing, and he was good with his hands; years of baking had given him that. With sex, he usually just got right down to business. But then, he didn't really know the other guys he'd been with. Being with Del again made everything different. He'd be willing to try whatever he wanted. "You know what else I like?"

"What?" Del's voice was low and rough. Del looked up, and for a moment the intensity was almost too much.

"My cock down your throat." The look in Del's eyes turned wicked again. Then he took Noah down all the way to the root.

Noah groaned and reached for him, hands sliding into his hair. Del worked his lips up and down Noah's shaft, and Noah let him control it, not wanting to hurt him.

When Del pulled off him to tease him again with the flat of his tongue, Noah looked down and held his gaze. "I want to come down your throat. I want you to take it all."

"Yes, please. I want that. I want you to use me."

Noah sucked in his breath. Holy shit, this was even hotter than his fantasies.

"Did I shock you?" Del licked along his length.

"I think I might need to… um…" Noah stumbled backward, reaching out blindly. He needed to sit down. Where the hell was the couch? Another step and he reached it and sank onto the cushions.

"Sit down?" Del asked, a cheeky grin on his face.

"That," Noah said.

Del walked on his knees until he was between Noah's spread legs. "Lean back and relax."

He did and Del took him down again. The heat, the

suction—it was too much. He tried to hold off, because he wanted this to last forever, but Del seemed to know exactly what he liked.

Del cupped his balls and tugged as he hummed around Noah's shaft. It was more than he could take. "Del. Del, I…"

Heat seared through him, and he came so hard, he thought he might pass out. He fought to stay conscious, though, because he needed to see Del's face as he swallowed, taking everything Noah had to give. It was the hottest thing he'd ever seen. Next time, he'd see how good it was if he pulled out and shot over Del's face. Would that be even better? Oh, fuck, he was imagining a future for them, a future where they kept doing this again and again, where they were lovers, where they could have forever.

DEL WIPED HIS MOUTH WITH THE BACK OF HIS HAND AS he stared at Noah. His head was flopped back against the cushions and his eyes were shut. Was he blissed out or feeling regretful? "Are you okay?"

"I don't know." Noah's voice was hoarse. When he opened his eyes, he looked more worried than satisfied.

Fuck. "Are you going to freak out on me?"

"No. Yes. I…"

Del rose to his feet and headed toward the kitchen.

"Don't leave."

The pleading in Noah's voice made Del's chest ache. "I'm not. I'm just getting you some water."

"Oh. Okay. Water's good."

But once he was in the kitchen, Del realized the timer must have gone off on the coffee cake. Fortunately, it wasn't burned. It looked done to him, so he took it out and turned the oven off.

He cut a piece for each of them, found plates and forks, and filled glasses with water. After placing everything on a tray, he headed back into the living room.

Noah hadn't moved, and Del wasn't sure if he was awake or not. "Noah?"

Noah blinked and then sat up. "Um… sorry."

"It's fine. I kind of like that I wore you out."

Noah seemed to notice the tray for the first time. "You brought cake?"

Del nodded. "The timer had gone off, but I think it's fine. You seemed like you might need a bit of sugar to revive you."

Noah still looked half-asleep. "I probably do, but you… what about… you didn't…"

Del smiled. "We'll take care of me in a little while." His cock protested that, but what was important right now was making sure Noah was okay with what had happened.

Noah frowned. "That's not fair."

"This was all about you, and I think that's actually very fair."

"So we're just going to sit here and eat cake instead of…"

He was adorable all mussed from falling sleep, and the fact that he cared, that he didn't want to be selfish… That gave Del even more hope. "Is there a problem with that?"

Noah looked him up and down. "Just that you're wearing too many clothes."

Del grinned. "So this is naked coffee cake time?"

Noah shrugged. "I feel weird being naked now if you're not."

If Noah wanted him naked, that's what he would get. He pulled his sweater off slowly, teasing Noah as he revealed inch after inch of his chest. He'd worked out hard to stay as fit as he'd been when he'd lived here and helped on the ranch. When his hand went to the button of his jeans, Noah cleared his throat. "Maybe that's enough for now, actually."

Oh hell, no. "I'm not stopping now. My cock might break right through the zipper if I don't get these off."

When Del pushed his jeans over his hips, his cock sprang free, and Noah moaned. God, Del loved that sound.

He got rid of his socks, shoes, pants, and briefs and joined Noah on the couch. "Now that we're both naked, let's try this cake."

Noah brushed his fingers along Del's hand as he took the fork Del held out to him, and Del had to resist the urge to press him back against the cushions and ravish him.

Focus on the cake. He took a bite of cake and groaned. "Wow. That's so good."

He looked up and caught Noah staring at him.

Noah coughed. "You… um… you looked like you really like the cake."

Del grinned. "I do."

Noah dropped his gaze to his own cake and took a bite. A few moments later, he glanced back up. Del hadn't been able to keep himself from watching Noah slide his lips over the tines of his fork. He obviously liked the cake too.

"You're doing it now."

Del shrugged. "I like watching you."

"You do?" He sounded more uncertain than Del would've expected. Did he really not know how badly Del wanted him, or how much he cared? There'd always been more than lust between them.

"I watched you all the time in high school. Every class we had together. I don't understand how no one noticed."

"I watched you too, but since almost everyone else was doing the same thing, either out of envy or longing, no one was going to make much of it."

Del took another bite of cake, and Noah's gaze drifted down. Del's cock jumped as if trying to draw attention to itself. He was hard and leaking, and he wanted Noah, but he wasn't going to push things. He wanted to let Noah set the pace.

"Del?"

"Yeah."

"I think we should eat this cake later."

"You do?"

Noah nodded.

"What should we do right now?"

"You should go get on my bed."

Del's heart pounded. This was what he wanted, but he was suddenly frozen with nerves.

"If you still want me to—"

"I do!" Del realized he was ridiculously loud, but Noah just laughed.

"You trust me to take charge?"

"I trust you completely, with everything."

Noah looked shocked by that. "After all that happened… After all this time, expecting me to be hurt and angry, you still trust me?"

Del nodded. It might not make sense, but he did. Noah wasn't the kind of person to seek revenge or to trick Del. If he wanted to hurt Del, he'd do it to his face, with words.

"I just… I hadn't expected that, but you're right. You can trust me. I'll take care of you. And if you change your mind, I'll stop, no matter how far we've gone."

Del had already known he would. "Okay."

"Bed?" Noah asked.

"Yeah. Bed."

He followed Noah into his room, growing more nervous with each step. He'd fantasized about being with Noah again so many times, but what if it wasn't like he remembered? He sat down on the edge of the bed, but he wasn't sure what to do next. "Um… How do you want me?"

Noah frowned, and Del was sure this felt just as awkward for him.

"I can just—"

"Maybe we shouldn't—"

Their words ran over each other and they froze for a moment. Then Del reached for Noah's hand. "Tell me what to do. That's what I want. You in charge. I want you to tell me what pleases you, and then I want you to fuck me until I beg for more."

Noah sucked in his breath. "Oh."

Del loved the look of lust combined with surprise. He could breathe now. Things were back on track.

"On your back. Hands over your head," Noah commanded.

Del obeyed immediately. Noah climbed on the bed and pushed Del's legs apart so he could settle between them. Then he ran his hands over Del's body from shoulder to thigh, making him shiver. He tried to stay still, but as Noah's hand came closer and closer to his cock, he couldn't keep from squirming.

"You like that?"

"Yessss."

Noah did it again, moving his hands more slowly this time and pausing to pinch his nipples. Del arched off the bed. "Fuck, that hurt."

Noah looked down at him, eyes filled with lust. "It was supposed to."

Now everything felt right. "More."

Noah took hold of his wrists and pinned them to the

mattress as he kissed him, softly at first and then hard enough to make Del squirm. He needed more, so much more.

"I wish you'd never left," Noah whispered against his lips when he pulled back.

"Noah, I..."

Noah sat back, and the look on his face told Del he was having second thoughts.

He propped himself up on his elbows and reached for Noah's hand. "Please. I need this. I think you do too."

Noah looked conflicted. "Will we regret it?"

"I won't. And I won't leave. Please."

Del groaned when Noah gave in and wrapped a hand around his cock. It felt so good, both the firm grip and the knowledge that Noah wanted him that badly.

"I bet you really want to come after waiting, don't you?" Noah asked.

Fuck yes he did, and Noah's slow strokes were making it worse. "Please."

"That's too bad, because I'm going to make you wait some more."

"You are?" Del couldn't take his eyes off his cock as Noah kept working it.

Precum dripped from the slit, and Noah shocked him by bending over and licking it up.

"More," Del begged, but Noah shook his head.

"You don't deserve more yet."

Del sucked in his breath. It was like Noah was reading his mind the way he'd seemed to in high school. "Please, Noah. Now."

"Don't move. I'm going to get some lube and a condom."

"Okay."

Noah ran into the bathroom and was back a moment later.

When he settled between Del's legs, Del could tell Noah was overthinking things again.

"Whatever you're thinking so hard about, just take it out on my ass."

Noah spluttered. "How did you know I… I don't want to be too rough."

Del shivered. "That's what I want, though. And I want to be yours. I want to… I don't know. I just want."

"Me too." Noah took hold of Del's legs and pushed until they were doubled on his chest. "Hold them. I want you spread open for me."

"Oh God. This is…"

"Good?"

"Yes," Del said as he stared up at him, feeling vulnerable but knowing that was what they both needed.

Noah slid his fingers over Del's ass. "This time, there's no hiding from me."

Del didn't want to hide anymore. He watched as Noah slicked up his fingers. When he teased the rim of Del's ass, he gasped.

"Like that?"

"Yes. Please." Del didn't even know what he was begging for. Just more. More of Noah any way he wanted to give himself.

Noah pushed his finger in and Del tensed. It didn't hurt exactly, but he couldn't help but stiffen.

"Are you all right?" Noah asked.

Del nodded. "I… um… I haven't bottomed since you."

Noah's eyes widened, but he didn't question him, he just caressed the back of Del's thigh with a soothing motion. "I'll go easy at first, okay?"

"I know. It's just. I want this, but I'm scared, not of it hurting—I'll be fine with that—but of what this means."

Del had been scared most of the time in high school, but he'd only admitted it to Noah once. He'd come out to his parents a few days before he left town. After talking to them, he'd gone to see Noah and cried on his shoulder while Noah held him. He'd been so afraid of what his parents would think of him if he admitted who he really was that he never gave them a chance to accept him before he left.

"Breathe," Noah encouraged him as he pushed deeper. Slowly, Del relaxed, and Noah worked a second finger into his body. When Noah pressed against his sweet spot for the first time, Del cried out, the sensation more intense than anything he'd felt before. He arched his back, desperate and needy. "Noah, please. More."

Noah chuckled. "Yeah It's time for more."

Del whimpered when Noah pulled his fingers from Del's body. He watched, cock aching and mouth gone dry, as Noah rolled on a condom and slicked himself up.

When Noah seemed ready, Del started to turn over so he could get on his hands and knees, but Noah grabbed his hip, stopping him.

"I want you on your back so you can look at me, and I can believe you won't run."

Fuck. He wasn't sure he could handle that. "Noah… I…"

Noah pushed him back against the mattress and ran a hand over his sweat-slick chest. "Do this for me."

He wanted to see Noah, to watch his expression as he pushed into Del. "Okay."

Noah teased him for a moment, circling Del's hole with his finger, then his cock was there, and he was stretching Del and—

Del clutched at Noah's shoulders. "You feel fucking huge."

Noah arched his brows dramatically. "Why, thank you."

They both laughed, which helped Del relax.

"Touch yourself," Noah commanded.

Del wrapped a hand around his cock and stroked a few times, but he froze when Noah pushed in farther. "This is… I don't…"

"I didn't tell you to stop jerking off." Noah was scowling at him, and it was so incredibly hot.

"I… That's…"

"Work your cock unless you truly want me to stop. I want to see how you jerk off when you're alone, when you want to get off fast."

Wow. Noah was so good at this. "I fantasized about you talking to me like this, but I didn't think you'd…"

"Now."

Del slid his hand up and down his shaft again, then began to move it faster. He could feel beads of sweat running down his face, and his breaths were raspy.

Noah pushed deeper. "Almost there. You're going to take all of me, just like you used to. Remember how you would beg me for it?"

Del whimpered as heat rushed to his face. He remembered. He'd jerked off to those memories again and again. Just like back then, he felt stretched to the limit, but he didn't want Noah to stop.

Noah stroked his cheek. "You're doing so good."

Any fear he'd had fled then. Noah reassuring him, letting Del know he was pleasing Noah, was the best thing in the world.

Noah pulled out slightly, then drove forward. Del cried out as Noah's hips met his ass. He was so fucking full. "I don't… I don't know if—"

"Breathe." Noah laid a hand on Del's chest. "Just breathe and look at me."

Del did.

"Are you okay?"

"I… yeah."

"Del?"

"It hurts, but I want it to." He'd said those same words when Noah had spanked him.

Noah exhaled as if he'd been holding his breath. "I wasn't sure I'd ever hear you say that again." He gave Del one long, torturously slow stroke. "You have to tell me if I go too far, because I want to remember how you look when you're so full of me you can't hold back, when you have to let go and just fall."

"Holy fuck!" Noah pulled out again, but this time he drove back in hard, making Del cry out. "Noah! Please! You can… Just please."

"You're so hot like this, but I don't want to hurt you."

"I don't care if it hurts. I need this. I need you."

Noah increased his pace, and soon he was driving deep into Del. Del thought he might lose his mind from the pleasure of it. He gripped Noah's shoulders so hard he'd probably leave marks as he worked his hips, meeting every one of Noah's strokes. He was so close, ready to come any second. His balls tightened, and every time Noah's cock slid over the sweet spot inside him, he thought he would lose it.

Noah reached between them and grasped Del's cock, working it with quick, sure strokes. "I want you to come now. I want to feel you shake. I want you to cry out as you give it all to me."

"Yes! Oh God, yes!" He made a strangled sound as his cock jerked and cum splashed his chest and coated Noah's hand.

His body spasmed again and again, his orgasm seeming to

last forever. When he was utterly drained, Noah let him go and pushed up on both arms. "Look at me."

Del did, and Noah held his gaze as he drove deep, fucking him relentlessly. Del was exhausted and sore, but it still felt so good. His cock jerked as if it wished it could go again.

"Let go, Noah. I want to see you."

Seconds later, he did, and the look of ecstasy on his face sent shivers through Del.

TWELVE

Several moments later, Del shifted, trying to slide out from under Noah so he could breathe.

"Sorry," Noah said, rolling to his side. "I'm usually not that out of it afterward."

Del grinned at him. "I like that I affected you that much." He'd liked everything about being with Noah, especially the way he'd taken charge and said such filthy things to Del.

When Noah slipped from his body, he winced. Damn, he was going to be sore, but it was so worth it. He sighed and let himself sink into the mattress while Noah stepped into the bathroom. It had been way too long since he'd done something just for himself. Noah made him feel like he could be his own person again.

"Are you really okay?" Noah asked when he returned.

"Yes. I feel better than I have in ages."

"Good, because I kind of lost it there at the end."

Del smiled. "I didn't mind. Actually, I loved it."

"So much that you stayed."

That hurt. "Noah, I told you I wasn't going to—"

Noah held up his hands in surrender. "I was joking. I'm sorry."

"I'm not ready to joke about me running, okay?"

"I'm sorry. I should've known that. Do you want cake now?" Noah pulled a pair of sweats and a t-shirt from a drawer and tossed them to him.

Del tried to reach for them but then he flopped back down. "I do, but I'm not sure I can walk."

Noah gave him a satisfied grin. "I suppose I should feel bad about that."

"But you don't."

"Nope."

Warmth filled Del's chest. He hadn't been sure he'd ever see Noah that happy again. "Good, because I want you to do it again. Soon."

"Then show me you can walk." Noah held out his hand, and Del took it.

When they were dressed and settled on the couch with more cake—Del had rejected the hard kitchen chairs—Noah said, "We're going to have to talk about this. About us and where we stand. I guarantee someone saw you come over here. They or someone else will guess what happened, or at least some of it. By tonight the whole town will know."

"And they'll deal with it."

"Del, it's not that simple."

"I don't think this is going to be easy, but I'm done with hiding, done with running. I told you that."

"You told me you came back because of Clarice."

He had, but that wasn't the whole truth. "Even if we'd stayed in Chicago, I was going to call you."

Noah raised his brows. "You really expect me to believe that?"

"After this? Yes."

Noah's chest rose and fell as he took a long breath. "All right. Maybe."

They ate their cake in silence for a few moments, then Noah said, "So where do we go from here?"

"Lunch?" Del knew it sounded like a flippant answer, but he didn't want to do any more soul-searching just then.

Noah closed his eyes for a moment, and Del imagined he was praying for patience.

"I mean a lunch date. In a restaurant. Here. In Anticipation."

Noah looked at him again. "You really mean that?"

"I do. I want to take you out to lunch."

"You mean you want to actually date me?"

"What did you think this was about?" Had this been a one-off to Noah? Had he just been getting Del out of his system? Please, God, don't let it have been a pity fuck.

"Us giving in to the fact that we want each other?"

"That's all? You didn't think we'd need more?" Why had he said that?

Noah frowned, looking as uncertain as he had before they'd fucked. "I wasn't sure you wanted more."

"When I said I wasn't going to run, I didn't just mean back to Chicago. I'm not running from any of this. I won't hide how I feel about you, and if you're willing to go out with me, I won't hide us."

Noah squeezed his eyes shut, and Del was sure he saw tears in them. "Maybe I'm not giving you enough of a chance."

Del took Noah's hands in his. "No, you are. More than you should, but—"

"You're really ready for that? To be out here?"

"Everyone already knows I'm gay."

"Knowing it and seeing you out with a man aren't the same thing."

He knew Noah was right, but he didn't want to analyze it. "You're right, but I am ready. If David and Oliver can do it, then I can too."

"Not everyone is okay with it, and they didn't grow up here."

Del wasn't going to back down. "I don't care what people say. I care about you and I want to be with you."

"And if it gets to be too much?"

"I'll find a way to make it work."

Noah clearly wasn't ready to believe that, and Del knew he couldn't convince him of it in one day. "Whatever the consequences, it will be worth it. You're the only man I've wanted like this."

"Like this?"

His pulse throbbed in his ears. "The only man I've ever seen myself staying with."

"You…? You're serious?"

"I am. I know I can't make up for what I did, but I still want to try."

Noah smiled. "You're off to a good start."

"Good. Now where should we go for lunch?"

"Pizza Palace? We'll see plenty of people, but it's not as gossipy as Jolene's Diner or the sandwich shop."

Nothing was as gossipy as Ida's sandwich shop. Most of the older women in town stopped in at least a few times a week for chicken salad and a full helping of everyone else's business. "Perfect. There's nothing like post-sex pizza."

"I suppose you still like your pizza with—"

"All the meat. Hell, yes."

"There so many jokes I could make, but they're just too easy."

Del laughed and pulled Noah to him for a kiss. "Thank you for giving me a chance."

Noah held him tight. "Don't make me regret it."

"I won't, but you're not going to believe that for a while."

"No, I'm not, but I want to." Noah stood and held out his hand. "Come on. We have to get dressed in real clothes."

"Wear those jeans you had on at the airport," Del said.

"You like those?"

"You know I do. You should always wear jeans that tight."

Noah rolled his eyes, but when he came out of the bedroom he had them on, along with a dark sweater that made his hair look even blonder. Noah hadn't had a clue how hot he was in high school, and Del didn't think he was any more aware of it now. That was one more thing Del hoped to change. Noah should understand just how amazing he was, inside and out.

WHEN THEY ARRIVED AT PIZZA PALACE, DEL'S CONFIDENCE began to fade. He was going to walk into a restaurant in Anticipation, Wyoming with his boyfriend. They were going to sit together. And people were going to know they weren't just there as friends, or at least they were going to assume it.

"Del, if you've changed your mind we don't have to do this."

Shit. He hadn't meant for his nerves to show so clearly. "I'll be fine." He wasn't going to back down.

"All right." Noah didn't sound convinced.

As they crossed the parking lot, Del wanted to reach for Noah's hand to reassure them both. He would have if he'd been in his neighborhood in Chicago, but he wasn't sure if

Noah would be okay with it here. Any public handholding they did would have to come later.

Lynnette was working the hostess stand. She and her husband ran the place. They went to Del's parents' old church. She'd taught him Sunday school when he was really young. Oh God, maybe he really couldn't do this.

"Del Crane, I heard you were back," she said as she grabbed a couple of menus for them.

"Yeah, I am."

"And you've brought a little girl with you?" she asked.

"My daughter, Clarice. She's at preschool now," he said, knowing an explanation was expected.

"Which one did you choose?"

"The Methodist church."

"Oh, Miss Molly will take great care of her."

She even knew which class Clarice was in. Lovely.

"So is it just the two of you today?" She looked around as if someone else might appear.

"That's right," Noah said, a hard edge to his voice.

Without further comment, she seated them in a booth and told them a waitress would be right with them. Jennie appeared at their table a few minutes later. She'd graduated with them, married another of their classmates, and was now very pregnant.

"How are you feeling?" Noah asked.

She sighed. "So tired. I'm so ready for this baby to come, but I've got another month to go."

He gave her a sympathetic smile. When she turned toward Del, her eyes went wide. "Oh my goodness. Is that really you?"

"It is."

"I heard you were coming back. Tired of the big city?"

"Yeah, a little bit." It was easier to just go with that.

"I bet. I don't know how you could stand it, but then I guess I've always expected to stay right here. Me and Ronnie have a piece of my parents' land, but we're still building up our operation, so I'm taking shifts here when I can. Not for long, though."

"That's good you have your own place and all."

"I guess it's not much compared to your family's ranch, but it's nice, and we'll have plenty of room for little Susie to run around." She rubbed her belly.

"So you're having a girl?"

"We are." She leaned in closer. "I probably shouldn't ask this, but I'm just dying to know. Is it true?"

"Is what true?" Noah asked.

"Are you two really—" She glanced back and forth. "You know."

"Gay?" Noah asked.

"Well, I know that, but are you together?"

Del wasn't sure what to say, because he didn't know if Noah really considered them to be or not.

"Yes," Noah said. There was no hesitation in his voice.

Jennie smiled. "Well, I think that's nice. I don't mind a bit. Ronnie, he's… well you know how men are. Uh… straight men, I mean."

Del just nodded. He could only imagine what Ronnie might say about his and Noah's relationship.

"Thanks, Jennie," Noah said.

"Well, yeah, I mean plenty of people round here don't mind. I just don't want you thinking you're not welcome or anything."

Del knew she was trying to make them feel better, but she was only making him more nervous. "I appreciate that. I think we want a meat lovers. A large one."

"Oh, right. I'm supposed get your orders, aren't I? No use

in coming over here otherwise. I can't remember a thing these days."

"That's okay." Del smiled at her, hoping he hadn't sounded too rude.

"So what do you want to drink?"

Del considered his options. Did he dare to order a beer at lunch on a weekday when most of the town would hear all the details of his date? Why the hell not? "I'll take a Blue Moon."

Jennie noted his order without any commentary.

"Same for me," Noah said.

"All right. I'll be right back, boys."

Del loved that she called them boys despite them being the same age and knowing Del had a daughter. He sighed. "Well, that was… Probably what I should've expected."

"Awkward, but not hostile?"

He nodded. "I know it will be harder some places, but this isn't bad."

Noah smiled at him. "It's really not."

Things continued to go well as the restaurant got more crowded and they waited for their pizza. A few people waved to them and a couple of others, including Del's cousin, the local children's librarian, stopped by to say hi. Everyone seemed more interested in asking about Clarice than questioning what he was doing with Noah.

Then Chad Waterson came in with Buck and Lewis, two of the guys Del used to hang with in school. Del had heard they'd opened a real estate business together and were responsible for some of the shitty developments that had been thrown up on the outskirts of town. They were also bigots and fancied themselves religious, except when that didn't suit them, like when they went to Casper to hit the strip clubs.

They were seated a few booths down from Del, but at least he wouldn't have to look at them. He hoped they hadn't noticed him and Noah, but that hope came crashing down a few moments later when, not bothering to moderate his voice, Chad asked Jennie, "Is that Del Crane over there? I heard that faggot was back in town."

"Del and his daughter are living at Crane Acres now," Jennie answered.

"How'd a fairy like that get a daughter?"

Jennie sniffed. "That's hardly my business."

"I reckon not. You got a real man."

"Del is just as real a man as Ronnie." Del knew Jennie really didn't mind him being gay, but he hadn't expected her to defend him like that. Maybe he should get to know her better.

Buck snorted. "That's a good one. Pregnancy really has rattled your brain."

Del pressed his hands to the table and started to stand, but Noah caught his gaze and shook his head as if he knew Del wanted to go over and punch Buck in his smug face.

"Do you know what you'd like?" he heard Jennie ask. The assholes ordered, and she walked away without looking toward Del and Noah.

"Do you want to go?" Noah asked, his voice low.

Del shook his head. "We're not done eating. I won't let them run us off." But despite what he'd said, he started eating faster, and he couldn't help noticing Noah did too.

"Do you deal with this all the time?" Del asked.

"I think everyone is used to me, and I hardly ever date anyone here." He sighed. "Okay, I never date anyone here. One gay man isn't much of a threat, but now with Oliver and David and you and me here, people will assume we're going to form some kind of gay coalition and start having sex in the streets."

Del would've laughed if it wasn't so damn sad. He looked

down at the pizza he no longer wanted. "I'm sorry. I didn't realize… I assumed you'd…"

Noah laid a hand over his. "I wanted to go out with you. I don't care what people think. There just hasn't been anyone special enough for me to bring home."

Del wished he didn't care what people thought, but it wasn't easy knowing a lot of people he'd grown up with now thought he was less than a man.

"I don't know what the hell they're doing here," Buck said loudly. "This ain't Chicago." Did he want them to hear, or did he just not know how to moderate his voice? Del wasn't a hundred percent sure.

"They shouldn't allow it. I don't want damn gays thinking they can spread their filth all over town." This sentiment came from Chad's other friend, Lewis.

Del considered going over there and telling them off, but Noah tightened his grip on Del's arm. "Don't. It won't help, and somehow we'll end up looking like the bad guys."

"But we shouldn't just let them say shit like that."

Noah glanced at Del's plate. "Are you done eating?"

"Yeah, I don't want any more."

"Me either. Let's get out of here."

"All right."

Noah signaled to Jennie. When she reached their table, Del noticed she looked pale. "Do you need to sit down?"

She shook her head. "No, I'm fine. I just…" She glanced toward Chad's table. "I'm sorry about that."

"It's not your fault," Noah said. "But we're ready for our check."

"I can tell Lynette. She'll ask them to leave. They're always offending someone in here. It's not just you." Del wasn't so sure about that. Lynette hadn't seemed thrilled about him being there with Noah.

"You don't have to do that. We were ready to go anyway."

"Are you sure?"

They both nodded.

"Okay."

The ride back to Noah's house was filled with awkward silence. Del wanted to reassure Noah that he wasn't going to take off because of a few assholes, but if he was honest with himself, a part of him was screaming for him to do exactly that.

When Noah put the car in park and cut the engine, Del fought back the panic that seemed to be closing in on him. Things were going to be ok. They had to be. He and Noah would find a way to make things work.

"I guess you probably need to go," Noah said, his voice flat.

Del wanted to say something, but he didn't know how to make Noah feel better when he was on the edge of freaking out himself. "I guess I should. I don't want to risk being late to get Clarice. She's still nervous about being at a new school."

"Yeah. You should be there early." Noah still didn't sound like himself.

Del had an idea. "You could come with me."

"To preschool pickup?"

He nodded.

"Do you really think that's a good idea?"

"Clarice would love to show you her school."

Noah seemed to be considering it, but ultimately, he shook his head. "Maybe another time."

"Noah, I'm not—"

"I need to think through what I'm baking this week."

"Oh, right. Well, I'll call you tomorrow."

"Yeah. That's good." They got out of Noah's truck, and he turned toward his house.

"Noah?"

He looked back at Del, and Del saw pain in his eyes before he covered it again.

"Those assholes aren't going to change my mind. I still want to be with you."

Noah gave Del the saddest smile. "Go on. Don't be late because of me."

He wanted to say Clarice would understand if he told her Noah needed him. Clarice cared about Noah too. Instead, he just got in his car and drove away.

THIRTEEN

Noah sank onto the couch and dropped his head into his hands. It was his own fault. He'd let Del in, literally and figuratively. Into his house, into his heart, into his dreams. And it had felt so good. So incredibly good.

He'd agreed to a take a new step with Del, to trust that maybe things really could work. Then Chad and his friends had to ruin it. The look on Del's face when Buck had said what he did had almost made Noah decide to skip town. Noah had thought he was used to being out in Anticipation. He'd convinced himself—probably because of his sex high—that going out with Del wasn't a big deal, despite knowing they'd face more prejudice as a couple. He'd heard some of the shit people had been saying about David and Oliver over the last few weeks.

Del said he could handle it. You freaked out more than he did.

Del had wanted to get the hell out of Pizza Palace as fast as he could. Noah was sure of that. And he could hardly blame the guy.

Stop assuming things are over.

Wasn't that the only way he could protect himself, though? If he started doing things like going with Del to pick up Clarice, he'd become even more entwined in their lives, which would make it even more devastating when Del decided this was all too much. Once Del smoothed things over with his family and became more confident being a dad, he would go back to Chicago or somewhere else, and Noah would be alone again. That was inevitable, right?

Noah could just hear his mother saying how he wasn't one to count his chickens before they hatched; he simply assumed none of them would hatch at all.

The more he thought about all this, the worse he felt. So he forced himself to get up off the couch and quit moping. He'd been planning to make bread that afternoon, so that's what he'd do.

A while later when he was punching down the dough after the first rise, his doorbell rang. His hands were covered in dough, so he just yelled "Come in." As the knob turned, he prayed it wasn't Del. He needed more time before he was ready to talk to him about their date.

Are you going to hide from him forever?

He was saved from answering his conscience by Marty stepping into the living room.

"Sorry I couldn't get the door," Noah said. "My hands are covered in dough."

"On your day off?"

Noah shrugged. "A day without baking is just not right." Was it pathetic that he didn't have anything else to do?

You could be with Del and Clarice right now.

Marty grinned. "I like to bake every day too. I was just surprised, since you do so much of it. I don't put in nearly the hours you do."

Marty helped Noah in the kitchen on Marie's day off, and

he did some of the baking on their busiest days, but he'd completely taken over making the lunch specials. Noah said, "You could do more if you wanted to, but what you really ought to consider is opening your own restaurant or catering business."

Marty gave a shy smile. "Thank you."

"Is that for me?" Noah inclined his head toward the foiled-covered container in Marty's hands.

"Yes. Your mom thought even if you didn't need lunch, you might still need dinner, so she told me to bring this over."

Of course she did. "What is it?"

"Chicken and dumplings."

"Yours?"

He nodded.

"Then I definitely need it." Marty was truly an amazing cook.

His face turned deeply pink, making him even more ridiculously cute than usual.

"Are you making bread?"

Noah nodded. "It's a rosemary and orange braided loaf I've been wanting to try out."

"Ooh, that sounds interesting. Do you need help shaping it?"

"Sure, if you don't need to get back."

He shook his head. "It's really slow today. Your mom said I could head home after I dropped this off."

"All right. I'm making two loaves, so if you braid one and I do the other, that'll be perfect."

Marty washed his hands, and Noah pointed to a cupboard. "There's an apron in there."

Marty pulled it out. He had to adjust it so it didn't hang halfway down his chest. He was probably only five seven or so and small framed. Perfectly twink-sized. With his long, curly hair and half-sleeve tattoos, he was attractive as hell, but Noah felt too much like his older brother for there to be anything between them.

"So… um… I heard you and Del went out today," Marty said as Noah finished kneading and began separating the dough.

"Wow, it's all over town already?"

"Yeah, I guess so, and I don't mean to pry or whatever. But if you need someone to talk to or anything, I'll listen."

The fact that Marty, who rarely talked about anything personal, was offering to be there for him sent all kinds of feels through Noah. "I don't want to make you listen to all my angst."

"Nah. I don't mind. I've been thinking about coming out, but… Well, I admire you because you have, and I want you to be able to date here. It's stupid what those bastards said."

When Marty had shared his sexuality with Noah and his mother, he'd asked them to keep it a secret. "Thank you, and if you do want to come out, you know I have your back. I don't know if brave is the right word for me, though. Stubborn might be closer."

Marty laughed. "Whatever it is. I still wish I had the courage to just be me, but when I first moved here, all I wanted was to feel safe. I didn't think announcing I was gay was the way to do that."

"I understand that completely." Marty had run from an abusive boyfriend, and he'd needed some time to get himself together. Noah was thrilled that they'd been able to offer him a job. "I'm not going to tell you what you should do now, but I will say that even though being out here isn't easy, I think hiding who I am would make me feel worse."

"Everyone assumes I'm gay anyway, because I'm small and… well, not masculine."

Noah had been guilty of making that assumption too before Marty had told him. “Assuming and knowing isn’t the same.”

“No, it’s not. Maybe eventually I’ll feel ready to be out.”

Noah smiled and handed him half the dough. They separated their halves into thirds, and Noah showed him how to begin the braid by pinching the ends together.

“I didn’t mean to make this all about me. I really do want to listen if you need someone,” Marty said as they pulled the dough pieces over and under one another.

Noah figured he might as well talk. He trusted Marty not to share what he said, and it might help to talk it through with someone. “I guess you know how Del left town after we graduated.”

“I know he left suddenly and didn’t come back, not even to see his mom and dad.”

“That’s right. He called home, and his parents visited him at school once or twice, but until a few weeks ago, he hadn’t been in Anticipation since the day he snuck off without telling anyone his plans.” Noah hated how bitter he sounded.

“And you… liked him?” Marty asked, keeping his eyes on his dough.

“I moved here at the start of high school, and Del and I became friends right away. We didn’t hang out much at school. He was popular, rich, sought after, and I was… not. I was The Gay Kid or The Weirdo. I had a few other friends, but no one I told secrets to like I did with Del when it was just the two of us.”

Marty frowned. “But he, like, ignored you at school?”

“It was more a mutual thing. I know it makes him sound awful, but it was honestly easier than trying to fit in with all the people who thought being around him made them cool.”

Marty nodded. “I guess I can see that.”

"All through high school I wondered if he liked me the way I liked him. I thought maybe he did, but I was never sure until the summer after graduation." Noah paused, uncertain whether to say more. He'd never told this to anyone, not even his mom, though he was sure she mostly knew what had happened.

"That summer we spent all our free time together, and it became more and more clear how he felt. He came out to me, kissed me, and I thought we were really going to be together. I thought we were going to make it work. He… he was my first."

"Oh, wow." Marty's eyes widened, and he sucked in his breath.

"The next day he was gone. He never returned any of my calls or texts."

"And you're still speaking to him?"

Noah sighed. "It's been five years. I've had a lot of time to process it all."

"So now you're dating him?" Marty winced as soon as the words were out. "Sorry, that sounded really judgy."

"No, I get it. I don't really know what I'm doing, but he's not the same guy who left. Having Clarice has changed him, and he swears he's staying here. He knows he screwed up and… Wow. Do I sound like an idiot for believing him?"

Marty shook his head. "You two were young, and he was scared."

Noah nodded. "He came out to his parents before he left, and I think that was part of why he ran. People kind of knew anyway, or they assumed—if you hang out all summer with The Gay Kid, people start to label you gay by association—but the idea of everyone actually knowing, of living here as a gay man freaked him out."

"And now he wants to go out with you, but on your first date you ran into Chad and his asshole buddies."

Noah nodded. "Right. So I don't know what happens now. I don't want to hope for too much."

"I saw how Del looked at you the other day when he came into the bakery, like you were the center of his world. I don't think hoping is wrong."

"Maybe, but I can't believe he's really going to stay, especially when so many people here will give him shit for who he is."

"Most people who come in the bakery seem okay with it; at least they're okay with you."

"They're okay with me when my being gay is an abstract idea. But if they see me with Del and have to confront that we're a couple?" Noah shrugged. "I don't know how that's going to go."

Marty laid a sticky hand over his. "I hope things work out for you."

"Thank you. I hope you figure out what's best for you too."

"Some days I'm really not sure what I'm doing in a little town like this. I just know I needed something different after… what happened."

"I'm glad you're here." Noah smiled at him.

"Thanks. I'm learning so much about baking and… well, life from you and your mom. I'm grateful you gave me a chance."

"You've got talent. I was serious when I said you could own your own restaurant." Damn it. Now he sounded like his mom.

Marty finished his braid and covered his loaf with plastic wrap so it could rise again. "Maybe someday. I don't know. Do you need me to do anything else?"

Noah glanced around. "No, we're all set, and I'm going to make some basic white bread for toasting, so there's no need to clean up."

"I guess I should get going, then." Marty untied his apron and laid it over the back of one of the kitchen chairs.

Noah almost asked him to stay, but he wasn't the best company. He would call him soon so they could hang out again. "Okay, but feel free to stop by any time."

"Yeah? Thanks."

"You're welcome, and if you want any more baking lessons, just let me know."

Marty smiled. "I'll do that."

After he left, Noah started the oven heating, so it would be at a nice even temperature when the bread was ready to go in. He looked at the two loaves on the counter. He wasn't going to be able to eat them both. He could bring one of them to Marty tomorrow, so he could give his opinion on the recipe. As Noah made himself a cup of coffee, he stared out the window and thought how much he wished he had someone to share moments like this with all the time. A partner. A husband. Del.

Just before bed that night, Del texted him a heart emoji. He sent one back, too nervous about the future to say anything else.

FOURTEEN

Close to noon the next day, Noah's phone rang, and he saw Del's name on his screen. His heart pounded as he accepted the call.

"Noah!" Clarice shouted.

"Hi, Clarice."

"Will you come watch me ride again today?"

Had Del let her call so Noah wouldn't be able to say no? Did he care? "What time should I be there?"

"You'll come? And you'll bring cupcakes? Daddy says it's at five."

He bit his lip to keep from laughing. Of course she had an ulterior motive. She was already so like her father. "I will come, but I'll have to bring some of what we have in the shop. I won't have time to make unicorn cupcakes."

"That's okay. I like all cupcakes. But not red ones."

He considered what was in the case. "How about chocolate with marshmallow cream filling and chocolate sprinkles on top?"

"Yes. Yes. Yes."

This time he couldn't restrain his laughter. "All right. Let me go so I can save some for you. I'll see you later."

"Wait. Daddy wants me to say you don't have to come if you don't have time, but I know you do."

He sighed. "I do, sweetheart. I'll be there."

"Okay. Love you."

God, his heart was melting. "I love you too."

"And Daddy?"

"What?"

"And you love Daddy."

Was Del listening? "I, um… Your Daddy is great."

"Yeah, he is. Most of the time. Bye." She ended the call, and Noah just stood there, staring at his phone.

"What's wrong? You're white as a sheet," Marie said as she walked through from the kitchen.

"Um… Nothing. I'm fine."

"You are not fine. Is something wrong with your man?"

Noah glanced around, but none of the people who were seated at tables seemed to be paying attention. "He's not my man."

"So that's why you went out with him. In town. When you never do that."

"I've been out of the closet here since high school."

She snorted. "Out, but never dating."

He almost asked how she knew that, but it was pointless. "There hasn't been anyone I wanted to date."

"All right. I'll buy that the pool of gay men in town is rather small—at least ones who are out. But you could've dated someone from Sheridan or Casper and occasionally brought them home."

"Del and I had lunch. That doesn't—" His stomach churned. It was a date, and he wasn't going to lie. Del didn't deserve that.

"You held his hand," Marie said.

Great, so all the details were being shared. "I guess you know what was on our pizza too."

"Meat lovers special and Blue Moon to drink."

Noah closed his eyes and took a slow breath.

"Um… I'm guessing that was a rhetorical question," Marie said, looking slightly contrite. "Why don't you take off early? I can handle the cleanup."

He almost told her to fuck off. He didn't need her sad attempt at apologizing for gossiping about him. But leaving now would allow him to shower and change before going to the ranch. "Fine, and you're running the register in the morning."

She sighed heavily. "All right. Deal."

Clarice looked even more pleased with herself than she had the first time he'd seen her ride Moon Pie. She'd apparently been practicing daily, and she actually had quite a good seat and a proper grip on the reins. She had the potential to be an excellent rider. By the end of the summer she might even be able to take some rides out with him and Del.

If they were still seeing each other. If she and Del were still there.

At least he could be sure that if she and Del left, Del would find her a place to take riding lessons. He might not be able to stand staying in Anticipation, but he would never deny Clarice's love of horses now that it was a reality rather than a fantasy.

Del glanced at him and smiled. Noah couldn't help smiling back despite the melancholy turn of his thoughts. Del was so proud of Clarice and not at all afraid to show it.

"She's really determined, isn't she?"

Del nodded. "She's always had a stubborn streak, but it translates to persisting with something whether or not it's easy."

"She makes it look like it comes naturally."

"I think that's because she's fearless."

Noah could see that. She hadn't been intimidated by even the largest horses, and when they'd driven out to look at one of the herds the other day, she would've walked right out in the pasture with the cows if Del had let her. As it was, she'd climbed up on the fence and tried to use it as a balance beam.

Noah had stayed right beside her and scooped her down when she wobbled. But Del made her promise never to do that again unless she held a grown-up's hand.

When Clarice's lesson was over and Del had coerced her into dismounting, Noah helped them untack Moon Pie and then curry and brush her.

As they were putting up the brushes, Clarice looked back and forth between Noah and Del. "Are you boyfriends?"

Noah nearly choked, and color rose in Del's face.

"We're… friends," Del said.

Clarice narrowed her eyes. "You tolded me you like boys, and Miss Molly told the baby room teacher Noah is your boyfriend."

Great. Teachers were openly gossiping about him at the preschool.

"I do," Del said. "I like boys the way some men like girls or um… women, I mean."

"I like your father a lot," Noah offered. "We're good friends, and maybe we could be more someday."

"Grandma said you took him on a date," she told Del.

Del sputtered. "She said that to you?"

"She said it to the phone."

Noah was relieved that at least Mrs. Crane hadn't told Clarice directly, but didn't she realize Clarice was always paying attention?

"You shouldn't listen in on phone conversations," Del said.

"But she was right there, and we were playing Candyland."

Noah turned away so Clarice wouldn't see him smile.

"We went to lunch together," Del said. "That's true. But you and I go to lunch sometimes, and that isn't a date."

Clarice seemed to consider this for a while and then nodded. "Okay, but I like Noah."

"I'm glad," Del said. "I like him too."

"It's okay if you want to be boyfriends."

"Thank you, sweetie. I'm glad you feel that way."

"Look, cows!" Clarice pointed to the nearest pasture where a cluster of cows were grazing. "Can I pet them?"

At least she'd dropped the topic of them dating.

"No honey, not now," Del said. "Remember, we only pet the cows when they're in the barn and an adult is with you."

"The baby ones are sooooo cute."

"They are." Noah squatted down beside her. "Watching them has always been one of my favorite things about spring."

"Do you want to come in?" Del asked.

"I don't think so. I…" He didn't think he could handle talking to Del's parents, not when he was so unsure where things were going. He stood and stepped away from Clarice.

"Are you sure?"

He nodded. "Yeah."

"What if I were able to slip out later?" Del asked, speaking so softly he was almost mouthing the words.

Noah leaned in close, lips nearly touching Del's ear. "To see your not-boyfriend?"

Del tugged him farther away from the fence. "You didn't want me to tell her, did you?"

"No, I don't think we're ready for that." Noah didn't add that he needed to be more certain Del and Clarice were really staying before they took that step.

What if they didn't stay? He could lie to himself all he wanted, but he was in love with Del, fully, heart-ready-to-burst-with-it in love. How would he survive if he lost Del again and Clarice with him?

What if Del asked Noah to move with him? Would he consider it?

Maybe.

His mother really would be okay. He could hear her now. *You need to stretch yourself. You need to do what's best for you for a change.*

But he truly liked it here, and he liked running the bakery. Yes, he could do more, and he thought maybe he would, but he didn't want to move. Hopefully that wouldn't be a decision he'd have to make.

NOAH GLANCED AT THE CLOCK AS HE PUT THE LAST BOWL IN his dishwasher. It was almost nine thirty. He needed to head to bed soon. Marie had the earliest shift, since she was making the next day's bread, but he still needed to be at work at five. Del hadn't texted him yet, so Noah assumed he'd either fallen asleep putting Clarice to bed—something he'd admitted to doing once or twice—or decided he didn't want to ask someone else to help if she woke up. Noah was fine with that. Clarice was adjusting so well to her new home, but she had to miss her mother. Del said she still had nightmares several nights a week.

They could find another time to be alone. Until now, he hadn't really understood how hard it was to have time alone as a parent, especially when you weren't living with your boyfriend… lover?… whatever. Not that Noah thought he and Del should move in together or anything. That would be…

Oh God, that would be perfect. So amazingly perfect. Going to bed every night wrapped around Del, having Del stretched out next to him in the morning, climbing on top of him, and—Great. Now he was going to have to jerk off before bed.

Someone knocked on the door.

Or maybe not.

He dried his hands and hurried to the door. When he saw Del through the peephole, he fumbled with the lock in his haste to open it.

As soon as Del stepped inside, Noah grabbed the front of his shirt and pulled him in for a kiss. All his worries about what to do, about whether he was going to end up more hurt than before, faded once Del was in his arms. When it was just the two of them, their heat and need for each other, nothing else mattered.

"Need you," he panted against Del's lips.

"Mmm. Need you too. I can't believe how long it took me to get you alone."

"You could've come over during preschool again," Noah said.

"I've had to put in a lot of hours to finish my current contract. I needed to work that day I came over, but I decided I didn't care."

"Del, you didn't have to—"

"I did, and I'm here now, so shut up."

Noah kissed him again. It was rough, full of tongues and teeth. Both of them seemed to want something they couldn't quite get.

Noah reached for Del's fly and worked the fastenings until he could reach inside and run his thumb over the head of Del's cock. He smiled when he found dampness there.

Del laughed. "I'm like this half the time just from thinking about you."

"Don't move." Noah undid his own pants and then took their cocks in one hand and stroked them slowly.

"Fucks, that feel so good."

"Kiss me," Noah demanded, and Del did. Noah kept his strokes light and slow, more a tease than an actual hand job. Del pushed into the circle of his fist, trying to get more friction, but Noah refused to give it to him.

"You're tormenting me," he gasped.

"And you like it."

"I like everything you do." Del slid his hand into the back of Noah's pants and teased his fingers along Noah's crack until he could circle the edge of his hole.

Noah couldn't go slow after that. He worked their cocks faster and faster, finally forcing himself to pull back when Del began to murmur incomprehensible things against his neck.

"Don't want to end it like this," he panted.

"Bed," Del said, grabbing his arm and tugging him toward the hall.

Noah looked Del up and down slowly and smiled when he saw Del shiver. "Do you still want me in charge?"

"Fuck, yes, I do."

"Then bend over the back of the couch. I don't want to go all the way to the bedroom."

Del grinned. "You might be even more impatient than me."

"Do what I said."

Del did, not even bothering to take his shirt off.

Noah had never been like this with anyone, never needed to fuck so badly he could hardly think. He usually managed to stay calm and controlled during sex. Maybe that was a sign he was never as into any of his partners as he was Del.

He yanked Del's pants down, exposing his ass, and Del groaned. "Why is this so hot?"

Noah chuckled. "I have no idea. But seeing you here, exposed for me like this, it's heaven." Noah caressed his ass and then gave it a light slap, and Del arched his back, sticking his ass out farther. "You want more?"

"Fuck, yes."

Noah spanked him harder, and he groaned. The sound was fucking beautiful. He kept going, bringing his hand down across Del's gorgeous ass cheeks again and again until they were bright red, and Del was panting. "More?"

Del whimpered.

Had he gone too far? He laid a hand at the base of his spine. "Breathe."

Del shook a shuddering breath.

"Are you okay?"

"So okay." The words were breathless, but Noah could hear the desire behind them.

He slapped Del's ass again, loving the way he jumped.

"Fuck, that—"

Another blow. Del whined and writhed like he wanted to escape. Noah spanked him two more times, once on each cheek, and then he rubbed the hot, reddened flesh.

Del shuddered.

"You're so fucking gorgeous like this."

"You… you mean that?" Del asked. He sounded close to tears.

Noah bent and kissed the imprints his hand had made. "I do," he whispered right against Del's ass.

"Thank you, Noah."

Noah had to squeeze his eyes shut for a moment to hold back tears. His hands shook as he stared at Del's gorgeous ass.

Del reached back and gripped his ass cheeks, pulling them apart. It had to hurt like hell, but he didn't act like he was in pain, he just begged, "Fuck me, Noah. Fuck me hard. I want to see if you can make this couch slide across the room."

"Don't move." Noah raced to his room to grab lube and a condom. If they kept this up, he'd need to stash some all over the house.

If Del moved in…

No, this wasn't the time to think about that. This was about sex, and that was one thing that was never an issue between them. Their bodies fit like they were made for each other.

He had the condom open before he got back, and he rolled it on as Del worked his hips against the couch.

"Lift up." He did and Noah placed a towel under him. "I don't want you damaging the upholstery. I paid at least fifty bucks for this gently used couch."

Del snickered against the sofa as he braced his arms on the cushion like he was ready to get pounded, but Noah wasn't going to make it that easy. He squirted some lube on his fingers and pushed two of them in. Del tensed, tightening until Noah's fingers ached.

"Relax. I'll take it slow if you need me to."

"No. Don't do that."

"What if it's what I want?"

Del unclenched his muscles, and Noah worked his fingers in and out, keeping a slow, steady rhythm. After a few moments, Del pushed back, trying to take more, but Noah wouldn't let him.

"Stop," Del begged, his voice ragged.

Noah did, pulling his fingers all the way out.

"No," Del moaned. "I mean stop teasing. I need more. I need…"

"What? Tell me what you need."

"I need your cock."

Noah smiled, loving that he'd forced that confession from Del. "You'll get it, but not yet."

"Noah, please!"

Noah squeezed his sore ass. "I'm in charge tonight."

Del gasped. "Hearing you say that is so fucking hot."

"Yeah, it is." Noah pushed his fingers back in and curled them so they teased Del's prostate.

Del twisted and squirmed, trying to take the digits deeper. "Again. Please."

When Noah did as he asked, Del bucked so hard he made the couch rock back on two legs.

"Keep the couch still, or I'll stop for good."

Del turned to him, wide-eyed. "You wouldn't."

"Are you so sure?"

"You need this as badly as I do."

Noah arched a brow. "I could put you on your knees and get what I want without ever touching you."

"Oh. My. God."

Noah smiled as he brushed the tip of his cock over Del's hole. "Promise me you'll be good and stay still."

"I… I don't think…"

Noah raked his nails down Del's back. "Promise."

"I'll stay still. I'll do anything. Just… please."

Noah pushed in, moving slowly but not stopping until their bodies pressed together. The friction had to hurt Del's ass, but he didn't complain, he just whimpered. Noah caressed his back as Del's body adjusted to Noah's invasion. "That's it. You can do this. You can take my whole cock."

"Noah!"

He pulled out and then pushed in again, harder this time. Del shuddered under him. "Can't. Can't stay still."

"Yes. You. Can."

A few more strokes and Noah was sweating, his cock so hard he was afraid he might come long before he meant to. It was all Noah could do to go slow enough to make sure there was a chance Del could obey. They were eventually going to break the couch. And he was okay with that.

"So good. You're holding so still." He ran his hand up and down Del's back. His skin was as slick with sweat as Noah's. "You know what I want now?"

"Wh-what?" Del's voice was strained with need.

"I want you to show me just how much you like this."

"But the couch."

"I'll get a new one."

"You're incredible."

Noah let go then, and so did Del. Their bodies slapped together as they unleashed their desire. The couch rocked and tipped and slid along the floor, but they ignored it as they pushed themselves harder, harder until Del cried out. "Close. I… Please let me come."

Noah reached under Del and stroked his cock. Seconds later, Del came, shooting cum toward the back of the couch and covering Noah's hand.

Del's climax seemed to go on forever. The pressure on his cock was almost more than Noah could take. The second Del was done, Noah drove deep into his ass and let go, filling the condom. When he sagged over Del's back a few moments later, the couch creaked ominously. He tried to stand, but before he could, the front corner crunched, and one of the legs gave way.

"Fuck," Del said.

"Worth it."

It took a bit for them to recover enough to move off the broken couch. Even then the room spun around Noah, but he managed to ease Del down to the floor where he curled on his side, obviously not wanting to sit after all Noah had done to his ass.

"Be right back." He hurried to the bathroom where he tossed the condom in the trash, cleaned himself up a little, and then brought a washcloth to Del. "Can you stay?" he asked once Del had wiped the cum off himself and pulled up his pants.

Del shook his head. "I have to get back in case Clarice wakes up."

Noah was disappointed, and he could tell Del was too, but he understood. "It's okay. This was… wow."

"More than wow. I wasn't sure you'd be willing to spank me again. I… I needed that."

"I think I did too. Everything seems so easy when…" Noah wasn't sure how to say what he meant without it sounding insulting.

"When you're taking charge of me like this?"

"Well… yeah."

"I know. Maybe one day things will be as easy with our clothes on."

"Maybe."

"Noah, I…"

Noah put a finger over Del's lips, afraid of what he might

say when he was probably still floating from his orgasm. "I'm not there yet."

"I know." Del closed his eyes, but Noah caught the hurt in them before he did. He just wasn't ready for words that might mean too much, words that might break him when Del left again.

Del pushed to his knees and then stood, so Noah did too. They both put their pants back on—Del wincing as he pulled his over his ass—and then looked at each other in awkward silence.

"So, um… Where exactly do we stand?" Del asked.

Noah kissed him then, softer than he had yet that night. He wanted the kiss to say the things he couldn't, the things that scared the fuck out of him.

"Taking things a day at a time?" he finally said when he forced himself to let Del go.

"All right. I just want you to know I wasn't scared off by Chad and his damn groupies. We can go out again anytime you want."

"I know we can." But Noah didn't make a suggestion for when or where.

Del sighed, and it made Noah's chest ache.

"Del—"

"It's okay, I'm not going to push you."

Noah knew it was wrong to be this intimate with Del—to have accepted his surrender, his trust, to have grabbed him the second he stepped in the door, pushed all his buttons, found ways to make him beg—and then refuse to go on another date or even to explain why he was scared. "I'm the one being an asshole now."

Del shrugged. "You deserve a turn."

"I don't think it's something you're supposed to take turns on."

"Just text me tomorrow. Okay?"

"Okay."

After Del left, Noah stared at his broken couch. He might be able to salvage it with some wood glue, but he wasn't going to worry about that now. He wasn't going to worry about anything. He was going to go to sleep, and maybe tomorrow he'd find the courage to either tell Del he was too scared to make this work or admit that he was in love with him.

FIFTEEN

The next morning, Noah texted Del good morning, and Del sent a heart emoji in reply along with a pic of Clarice with a huge smile on her face and a string of emojis from her. For nearly a week, his contact with Del stayed limited to texting, one brief call where Clarice took the phone and did most of the talking, and a quick hello when Del brought Clarice to the bakery for a cupcake. Noah felt guilty for being thankful the bakery was slammed so he could use that as an excuse not to sit down with them. But he still wasn't sure what to say. He loved Del, he was sure of that, but it terrified him. He didn't ever want to hurt like he had those first months after Del left town.

On Friday morning, David stopped by the bakery while Noah was restocking the pastry case.

"What are you up to today?" Noah's mom asked as David studied the day's offerings.

"Oliver and I were supposed to go look at a house, but one of his deadlines got moved up, so I'm going to go on my own."

"Noah could go with you," his mom said.

Normally, Noah hated when his mom attempted to make him be social, but he was ready to come out of his skin. Baking usually soothed him, but after days of agonizing over what to do about Del, nothing took his mind off it anymore.

"Are you sure you don't need me this afternoon?"

His mom shook her head. "We'll be fine, maybe better."

"Better?"

"You have to admit you've not been in the best mood today."

He hated that she was right. "Great, now David's not going to want me along either."

David laughed. "I'm sure the fresh air will be good for you."

"You always say that."

"Because it's always true."

Noah just rolled his eyes. "What time should I meet you?"

David glanced at the clock on the bakery wall. "I need to leave in about half an hour."

"All right. I'll go home and get changed and you can pick me up there."

When David arrived, Noah was braced for more questions about Del. He'd already debriefed with David and Oliver about seeing Del again after so many years, but today he needed to get away, not be forced to analyze things.

David must have sensed that because he just talked about the different properties he and Oliver had seen so far. For years, he'd wanted to own enough land to keep horses and possibly some other animals, and Oliver had convinced him to start looking now. Oliver had a lot of savings, and he was eager to give David what he wanted. As they walked around the property, checking out the house and the barn, Noah imagined himself and Del there. They could have horses and he could bake in the big farmhouse kitchen and—

"What do you think?" David asked.

He sighed. "It's perfect."

"For me—or for you and Del?"

"Both," Noah said automatically. Then he realized what he'd done. "Fuck."

"When are you going to tell him how you feel?"

"I don't know, I—"

"Remember what you told me when I was driving Oliver back to the lodge so he could fly home to Florida?"

Noah took a deep breath and rubbed at his temples, feeling a headache coming on. He'd scolded David for letting Oliver walk away without sharing his feelings. "Yes, dammit."

"Then follow your own advice."

"How can I—"

"Risk losing him again? I have no idea."

David was abso-fucking-lutely right. "Thank you."

"You're welcome. Now let's get you back so you can put your plan in action."

"Only if you promise to seriously consider buying this farm."

David looked around at the house and barn and then across the fields toward the gorgeous view of the mountains. "It's a deal."

NOAH HAD DAVID DROP HIM OFF AT THE BAKERY. THEY WERE about to close for the day, but he stirred up a batch of chocolate cookies with chocolate chunks, sprinkled them with sea salt and baked them just enough to leave them soft and gooey.

His mom came into the kitchen after the cookies had

come out of the oven. "Those look amazing! Can I have one?" She was already reaching for one as she asked.

"Sure, but they're—"

"Hot. Really hot."

Noah couldn't help but laugh as his mom jumped around making funny faces while trying to swallow a scorching bite of cookie.

"Still good, though, and so chocolatey. Are they for Del?"

Of course she'd guess. "Yes."

"Good." She took another, more careful bite.

"Why is that good?"

"Because you've been avoiding him."

And of course she'd see that too. "I haven't."

She raised her brows and glared at him.

"All right, fine. I have."

"Is it because of what happened at lunch?"

He shrugged. "A little bit."

She took another bite of cookie. He knew she was waiting for him to say more.

"I thought things were… I thought we could be okay."

"Did he say you couldn't be?"

"No, but if that's what it's going to be like whenever we get together…"

"You both know Chad, Buck, and Lewis aren't fit company for rats, much less humans."

"But Del isn't used to—"

"Do you think there aren't any homophobes in Chicago?" His mother gave him her I-didn't-raise-an-idiot look.

"No, but—"

"Del isn't that thin-skinned."

"But if that happened the very first time we went out, what might happen next time?" Noah asked.

"Is that really what this is about, or is this just you sabotaging something before it has a chance to start?"

Noah rolled his eyes. "Not that again."

"It's what—"

"I did with my culinary career. I know you think I screwed up."

His mom scowled. "I do not think that. I think you're amazing and caring and completely capable of making your own choices. I just don't want to hold you back, and I don't want you to hold yourself back either."

Noah sagged against the counter, feeling like a deflated balloon. "That is what I've been doing, holding myself back. But I don't want to get hurt."

"Is avoiding Del really going to prevent that?"

Noah knew nothing would keep him from getting hurt if Del walked away again. "It would be easier if I didn't… If this wasn't…"

"If you weren't in love with him?"

There was no point in denying it. "Yes. I wish I could just stop feeling like I do. Why do I still love him after all this time?"

"That's not how love works, honey. You can't just turn it off." She pulled Noah into her arms and hugged him tight.

Before they pulled apart, Noah kissed her cheek. "You've never held me back."

She started to protest, but he held up a hand. "Yes, I partly stayed here because I wanted to be close if you needed me, but I also stayed because I honestly love it here. Anticipation would be perfect if I didn't have to worry so much about people judging me, especially if I want to actually date someone."

"Then stay here and date and see how it goes. The important thing is that you allow yourself to take risks, with Del and with your baking."

She was right. He'd been holding himself back for far too long. "If you're okay here for a little while, I'm going to pack up these cookies and go take a risk right now."

She snatched another cookie.

"Hey!"

"That's my payment for doing cleanup today." She grinned at him and ruffled his hair, then headed back out front.

Noah's hands shook as he placed the cookies in a box. He could do this. Del wanted more and so did he. Things were going to be fine.

"At least you didn't forget how to ride while you were gone," Harvey said as he and Del reined in their horses. They were riding out to check on the herd, something Del used to love doing when he was a kid.

Del snorted. "Of course I didn't." He had actually been a little worried. He hadn't been on a horse since he'd finished college—he'd kept up his riding during those years by leading trail rides on a ranch in Iowa during the summers—but getting on a horse felt as natural as it had years ago when he'd lived there. He was glad he'd accepted Harvey's invitation to join him.

"I wish Dad had been able to come with us. How bad are things?"

Harvey sighed. "He'd be better if your mother would quit pestering him and making him sit all day."

"He really is going to be fine, though? He'll make a full recovery?"

"Yes. It was touch and go there for a bit, don't get me wrong. The doctors thought they might have to take his leg, but he's on the mend now. Hopefully he'll remember how to ride as easily as you."

Del smiled. His dad loved horses; he always had. "I'm sure he will."

They walked their horses in silence for a bit, studying the cattle. Eventually, Del broke the silence. "It was bad after I left, wasn't it?"

Harvey nodded. "Your mother didn't know whether to cry or throw things, and your dad spoke even less than usual. He'd ride out and not come back all day. When anyone asked him about you, he basically ignored them. For the first month or so, he stayed home almost as much as he has with his injury, because he didn't want to answer questions."

"He was embarrassed, wasn't he?" Del hated to even think about that.

Harvey shook his head. "No, it was more that he wasn't sure what to say. I don't think he would've chosen for things to be the way they are, but neither of them would have sent you away. Your mother didn't go out much either, and she didn't host any parties for six months."

That made Del freeze. He must have gripped the reins too hard because Goldie shied. "It's okay, girl." He patted her neck. "We're fine."

Del couldn't wrap his mind around the thought of his mom withdrawing like that. He'd had no idea how badly he'd hurt her.

"It's probably not my place to say," Harvey said. "But I think you owe your parents more of an explanation about why you ran. They may say they understand, but I'm not sure they really do. At least, they don't get why you couldn't have at least told them you needed to get out of town or why you never visited."

"Once I was gone, I built up how bad it would be to come back. And after a while, I didn't know if they'd want me here."

Harvey frowned. "Did you really think—"

"I was wrong, okay? I know that."

"Did you apologize?"

"I did, but I think you're right. I need to talk to them more." He'd been wanting to avoid it, hoping things would naturally start to feel easier between them, but he knew better.

"They're probably about to eat lunch now. I'd be happy to let Clarice help me in the barn when we get back if you want some time alone with them."

"You would?"

"Of course. She's amazing, so like you at that age."

Del winced. "Yikes." He hadn't been an easy kid.

"That doesn't mean she'll be quite as much trouble."

"I hope not."

"You're doing a great job with her," Harvey said. "And it wouldn't hurt if she saw a little more of your man."

"I don't have a—"

Harvey gave him a don't-bullshit-me look. "Noah is just as much your man as he was before you left."

"He doesn't trust me."

"Well I can't blame him, but since you're staying you can earn that trust. It doesn't have to happen immediately."

"No, I guess not." But he wanted it to. He wanted Noah so badly and not just sexually. He wanted more time to be alone with him. He wanted to belong to him. He wanted… forever.

"But just remember. If you run again, you might not be welcomed back."

It hurt that both Noah and Harvey doubted he would stay.

"I'm not going to run."

"That's good to hear, because you've seemed awful skittish the last few days."

Del blew out a long breath. "That's because I'm not sure Noah is willing to take a risk on me, and I'm not sure how to make things better with my parents, and… yes, it's hard being back. I feel like everyone's judging me, even though they probably judged me much more harshly back in high school when I was a rich, arrogant asshole who thought everyone existed to do his bidding."

Harvey shook his head. "You were never that bad. There were always people you cared about, even if you didn't know how to show them."

"Thanks for being here for me, now and before."

"You're a good kid. You always have been. You just need to believe it."

Was that really all he needed? To believe he could stay, that he could be a good dad, a good son, a good enough man for Noah. If so, maybe there really was a chance for him here.

NOAH PARKED NEAR THE SIDE DOOR OF THE RANCH HOUSE. When he knocked, Ella opened it and ushered him inside. "Del rode out with Harvey a while ago, but they should be back soon if you want to wait."

He wasn't sure he could sit still. His heart was racing, and his skin felt all buzzy. But if he left, he might never get up the nerve to come back. "Sure. I'll wait. Thank you."

"Can I get you something to drink: tea, coffee, beer?"

"I'm fine, thank you."

"Well at least sit down." She gestured toward the bar. "I've missed having you in my kitchen."

He'd missed her too. He set the Main Street Bakery box on the table. "I brought cookies."

She glanced in the box. "Oh, Del will love those. I think he still loves chocolate as much as he did as a kid."

Noah smiled. "That's great, but these are for everyone. Go ahead and have one if you want."

"Al right. Dinner's going so I can actually rest for a minute." She poured herself a cup of coffee before sitting down and taking a cookie from the box.

"What are you making?"

"Chicken parmesan."

"Mmm. That sounds great," Noah said.

"I'm sure you'd be welcome to stay."

Heat rushed to his face. "I wasn't angling for an invitation, but I do miss your cooking."

Ella beamed at him. "You're such a sweetheart."

Before Noah could respond, the sound of Mrs. Crane's voice floated in from the hallway. At first Noah thought she was talking to Ella, but then he realized she must be on the phone.

"Yes, he got the job… The one in Los Angeles… Right, so he'll probably head out there in a few weeks… Yes… We'll just have to rearrange our plans, but I'm happy for him… No I don't think he will."

Noah didn't hear anymore. His pulse was beating too loudly in his ears, drowning out her voice.

Job. Los Angeles. Going out there. She had to be talking about Del, though wouldn't she be sadder that he was leaving? Maybe she was. She was using that brittle everything-is-lovely tone she'd often used when Noah knew she'd just as soon tell him to fuck off.

He pushed back from the table. "I… um… I should be going."

"You're not going to wait for Del?" Ella asked.

"I… no. I shouldn't."

"Noah? What's wrong?"

"I just need to…" He couldn't get any more words out. He hated to be rude to Ella, but if he stayed any longer, he might have a meltdown right there in the Cranes' kitchen.

He ran for his truck and drove away like he'd just robbed the place and the cops were on his heels.

SIXTEEN

Del called for Clarice as he and Harvey stepped into the mudroom.

"Delford Crane, how many times have I told you not to shout in this house?" his mother said, making him feel as if he were six again.

"Sorry, Mom. Harvey needs Clarice's help in the barn, and our shoes are all muddy."

"Then take them off. That's what mudrooms are for."

Instead of the argument he wanted to make, he simply said, "Yes, ma'am." He wasn't actually six anymore. He could let things go.

"Daddy! Daddy! Guess what?" Clarice shouted as she ran toward them.

"What, princess?"

"I maded this!" She held out a roll.

"You did? With Ella?"

She nodded vigorously. "Grandma helped too."

He glanced at his mom, hoping his shock wasn't too evident. The idea of his mom working in the kitchen with their cook was almost beyond comprehension.

"Isn't it beautiful?"

He smiled. "Yes, sweetheart. Very beautiful." He took a bite. "And delicious."

"I already ate two."

"Did you?"

She nodded, looking quite serious, and he had to bite his lip to hold in a laugh. "Listen, I need to talk to your grandparents for a while. It will be boring grown-up talk, so Harvey thought you might like to help him in the barn."

Her eyes lit up. "Are we going to feed the horses?"

Harvey grinned. "Yes, we are."

"I love it here, Daddy!"

"I'm glad you do." How could he even think of leaving when Clarice was so happy?

"Come on," Harvey said. "Moon Pie will be thrilled to see you."

Clarice bounced out the door, not even remembering to run back and grab Uni from where she'd left him on the floor in the den.

"What's this about needing to talk to us?" his mother asked.

"I just have some things to say. Things I should've said the first night." Or years ago.

"All right, then. Your father was watching Clarice."

Del's heart pounded as they stepped into the den. His father looked up from a newspaper he was reading.

"Put that down, Edward," Del's mother said. "Delford wants to talk to us."

"Oh, all right, but I was—"

"Dad, it's kind of important."

"Oh, sorry." He laid the paper aside.

"Well, sit down, Delford," his mother said, doing so herself. "I don't want you hovering while you talk."

"I'm sorry for hurting you both." Del knew he had to get the words out fast if he was going to do this. He sank into a large upholstered chair and continued. "I know I said that before, but I didn't understand what it was like for you when I just disappeared. I know I should have talked to you about why I couldn't stay. I let you think I didn't care about you, and that's never been true, but once I'd been gone for a while, I was scared you wouldn't want me back or that I'd talk myself into returning for good, even though I thought I would be miserable here."

His mother started to protest, and he held up his hand.

"I wasn't miserable because of you, but because I couldn't be me here."

"Can you do that now?" his father asked.

"I think so."

His mother frowned. "And does being you include dating Noah?"

"Ada, we've already talked about how that's not our business."

She huffed, but she didn't say anything else.

"We should've seen how hard things were for you, son," his father said. "We knew something was wrong. Then when you told us what had been bothering you, we thought things would get better."

"I wanted them to. Noah and I…" Dear God, was he really going to say this? "I came out to him before I told you. I'd realized I was in love with him, and—"

"Did he hurt you?" Del's mom asked.

"No! He was amazing. He's the one who got me through the last years of high school. I don't know how I would've handled realizing I was gay if it weren't for him. And before you ask, he never influenced me. I knew I was gay before we became friends."

"I wasn't going to say that," his mother insisted. "I never… Well, even if I wondered about it, I realized it couldn't be true."

"It took us a while, son. It took some praying and some talking to people like Father Jackson, but eventually we understood as best we could."

"Wait. You went to the Episcopal church?" His father had always said the Episcopalians only cared about showing off their clothes and beating everyone else to Sunday brunch.

"We didn't go to their service, but we knew Father Jackson was all right with"—his father waved his hand around—"all this, so we thought he'd be a good person to talk to."

Del wished it weren't hard for his father to just say "being gay" or "gay rights" or something like that, but he was trying. "So did he help?"

His father nodded. "You might want to talk to him yourself one day."

Del was starting to feel like he didn't know his parents at all. How many things had he been wrong about? "I had no idea. That you were doing that, talking to people, or that you… that you were sad."

"You really thought we'd just go on with things after you left?" his mother asked.

"I thought—I thought you'd be angry."

"Oh, I was," his father said. "I was furious that you'd do that to your mother and me, but then I just missed you."

That nearly broke Del. "I'm so sorry. It took me way too long to grow up and realize I'd been an asshole to everyone."

"Del." His mother tsked. "Watch your language."

His father rolled his eyes. "I think that's the least of our problems right now, Ada." He turned to Del. "We're sorry you didn't think we were there for you."

Was this a time to be honest or to just soothe? His dad was being honest, and part of the reason things had gotten to this point was because Del hadn't been comfortable telling them how he felt years ago.

"I felt like you were too wrapped up in the ranch sometimes to think about what my life was like, and Mom was more concerned with my manners and my grades than how I felt." She started to protest, but he kept going. "I know I was a teenager, and I probably saw things the wrong way, but—"

"No. I don't think you did," his father said. "Not all the time, anyway. I love this ranch, and I want it to be something you're proud of too. But I didn't mean to make you think you came second to a herd of cattle or a barn full of horses."

"I didn't, not really, and I am proud of the ranch. I missed it so much I ended up leading trail rides in the summer."

"Where?" his father asked.

"On a dude ranch in Iowa."

His mother looked even more hurt by that. "Why didn't you just come home?"

"Because I couldn't face you after I'd screwed up so badly. And I couldn't be what Noah wanted me to be."

"If he wants you to change who you are, then—"

"He doesn't want me to change who I am, but he didn't want to date someone closeted, and I wasn't willing to be out in Anticipation back then."

"And now?" his mom asked.

"Now, I'm out by default, but he's struggling to believe I won't run off again."

His father nodded. "I can see why he'd worry about that."

"Edward, that's not—"

"The boy ran once after… well, I think I can imagine what happened."

"Dad!"

"I'm not as dumb as you think."

Del groaned. Did he really deserve this? "I don't think you're dumb."

"Well, you did when you were eighteen."

"Unaware, maybe, but not dumb."

His mother snorted. "As if you were aware of anything outside your own high school world."

Del took a slow breath. Her words hurt, but she wasn't wrong. "I didn't realize how much I was hurting you when I left. And it's true I thought about myself way too much."

His mother nodded. "You should have talked to us about how you felt."

"I tried."

"You told us off and—"

"Ada, can we just accept that the boy is sorry?"

She opened her mouth to say something else, then closed it and nodded.

"So I really do still have a place here?"

His mother's mouth dropped open. He didn't think he'd ever seen her gape like that. "Have a place here?"

"Yes." Was she going to ask him to leave after all?

"Delford Crane. This is your home. This will always be your home. It doesn't matter who you go out with or what you do. We would never…" Her voice cracked, and she dabbed at the corners of her eyes.

"We're your family," his dad said. "I think maybe you forgot that."

He had. He'd forgotten it a long time before he left town. Tears stung his eyes. "Thank you. I really am so very sorry."

His mother drew him into a hug and held on tight, tighter than he remembered her doing since he was really small.

His dad pushed his way to his feet.

"Dad, you don't have to—" His dad wrapped his arms around Del and his mother.

"This damn leg is never going to work right if I keep sitting around. The doctor says I need to move more and start putting more weight on it."

"Edward, he said a few minutes a day, and you've already been out in the barn and riding all over the country and—"

"Don't listen to your mother. She'd keep me right here all the damn time just so she has someone to talk to."

"I have Clarice to talk to now, and she doesn't bury her face in the ag report." Then his mom turned back to Del, suddenly composed again. "Oh, I meant to tell you."

Del tensed. Those words were often the prelude to her asking—telling, really—him to do something he did not want to do.

"Noah stopped by right before you got back to the house."

"He didn't stay?"

"No, he dropped off some cookies, and Ella said he took off in a hurry, acting like something had rattled him."

Del and Harvey had seen a truck tearing down the driveway as they'd approached the house. They'd wondered who it was, but the dust the vehicle had kicked up kept them from seeing much of anything. Had that been Noah? Why would he rush off like that?

"Did you talk to him?"

"I did not run the boy off, Del."

"But you don't really approve of him."

She sighed. "I had an idea of what your future would be like, and it wasn't… look, I'm trying, okay? If Noah is who you want to be with, then I'm okay with that."

Del knew that was the best he'd get for now. "What would've made him leave?"

"I have no idea. Maybe he realized something he needed to do?"

That didn't sound right. Wouldn't he have at least texted Del if he did? "Do you mind if I go talk to Ella?"

"Of course not, but we'll be eating dinner soon. I hoped you'd stay."

"I will." He couldn't refuse her, not now, but he could go see Noah after dinner.

"Did you have a good talk with your parents?" Ella asked when he stepped into the kitchen.

"I did, and dinner smells amazing."

"Thank you." She beamed at him, and he gave her a hug as he snatched another one of the rolls she and Clarice had made.

"Hey!" She slapped at his arm with a towel. "Just because I'm thrilled to have you back doesn't mean I've changed the rules of my kitchen."

They'd been playing this game of him stealing food and Ella pretending she cared since he was a kid. He would've thought it would feel stifling to fall back into patterns from his childhood. Instead, it comforted him.

"Mom says Noah came by and then left in a hurry."

"He did. He sat down with me while I was trying one of his cookies and having some coffee. I thought we were going to chat. Then your mother walked in while she was talking on the phone, and he started acting very strange. He basically ran away, and I have no idea why."

"Who was Mom on the phone with?"

Ella shrugged. "A friend of hers, I think, but I don't know for sure."

"And she didn't say anything to Noah?"

"Not a thing. All she did was wave to him when she realized he was here."

He considered calling Noah, but if Noah was upset about something, he wasn't likely to talk about it over the phone. If he tried to leave right after dinner, Clarice would insist on going too. He'd have to wait until after he got her settled for the night.

SEVENTEEN

Noah jumped when someone knocked on the door. He hadn't heard a car pull up or anyone come onto the porch. *What time is it?*

Only eight thirty. It felt so much later than that, probably because he'd just been lying on the couch feeling sorry for himself and watching movies for the last several hours. He hadn't bothered with dinner, unless you counted a few glasses of whiskey. He was also fairly sure he'd dozed off after giving in to the urge to cry at the end of *Notting Hill*.

"Noah? It's me. Del."

Oh, shit. Was he here to announce that he was leaving? At least that was better than running away. Or was it? Noah was no longer sure, but he knew he wouldn't make it through Del explaining how he got an opportunity somewhere else without either yelling at him or dissolving into tears.

"Noah? Are you okay?"

If he didn't answer, Del would call his mom. And facing a worried mother would be even worse than facing Del. So he pulled himself off the couch and finger combed his hair, hoping he didn't look as bad as he feared.

"I'm coming." With careful steps he made his way across the room. Whatever sleep he'd gotten hadn't been enough to sober him up.

He cracked the front door and stood there instead of offering for Del to come in. "What is it?"

Del gave him an odd look. "Ella says you ran off, but she doesn't know why. I came to check on you."

"And you don't have any idea why either?"

"No, should I?"

Noah bit back the words he wanted to shout at Del. "Look, it's a bad time, can we talk later?"

"A bad time. Why?"

"Do I have to tell you everything?"

Del flinched and took a step back. "No. Of course not. But if you've decided… If you've made up your mind about us… I wish you'd tell me."

"It sounds like you're making it up for me." So much for holding back.

"What?" Del looked baffled. Did he really not get it?

"I'm tired. I should just…"

"Can I please talk to you?"

"Fine." The room spun, making Noah nearly lose his footing as he moved back from the door. "I think I'm drunk."

"Yeah, I think you are."

"Well, I had to do something."

"*Do* something? About what?"

Noah took a step and leaned precariously to the side. Del caught his arm and guided him to the couch, which Noah had fixed to be more or less sturdy again.

"I know it would be better to talk when you're sober, but I need to know what happened. Did my mom say something to you?"

Noah shook his head and then regretted it. "Not to me."

"Did something she said on the phone upset you?"

"Can't you just tell me? Do you really have to string me along like this? It's not funny, you know."

"Tell you what? Noah, I really don't understand what's going on."

"So you're just going to pretend like you don't have a new job. You're going to sit there and act like you're not leaving. Do you know what it was like to hear that from your mom instead of from you?"

"Oh my God."

"Were you going to run again, or did you plan to tell me sometime? A few hours before you left, maybe? Because that's so much better than just disappearing."

Del shook his head. "You heard my mom say something on the phone, and you created a whole scenario about what it meant. You could've stayed and asked me about it instead of just assuming you knew what was going on. You never even gave me a chance."

"No. I couldn't have stayed. I could hardly speak, hardly think. That's what you've done to me. Don't you get it? I tried to fight it, but the minute you returned we were right back to where we were at eighteen with me in love with you but unsure what you're willing to give."

"I've told you again and again that I want to give you everything."

"All the way from Los Angeles?"

Del shook his head and ran a hand over his hair. "Do you understand what I do for work? Have you listened at all when I've talked about my contracts?"

"You work for a financial consulting firm and businesses contract your services." What difference did it make what he did if he was leaving?

"That's right, and I do have a new contract with a firm in

LA. I will have to fly out there for a few weeks to learn more about their business, but I'm not moving there. We work with companies all over the country. That's why I can do my job from here. I only need to be on location at the beginning of the contract and when I present my final plans."

Oh God. What had he done? "But… But you didn't say…"

"I didn't tell you because I just found out earlier today, and I won't be going out there for several weeks."

"Shit, I really screwed this up." Noah's head swam, and his vision began to go dark at the edges. Was he going to pass out?

"Yeah, you did. Why would you assume…? Do you not understand that I have changed?"

"I… I don't know."

"You don't know if I've changed, or—"

"I don't know if I can ever believe it."

Noah regretted the words as soon as he said them. Del stumbled back, pain evident in his eyes. "If there's nothing I can do to convince you, then I don't know what to say."

"I should have asked you about the job," Noah said, his voice trembling. "I know that, but I panicked. All I could think about was how pathetic I was for letting myself fall for you again."

"I've never gotten over you, Noah. Don't you see that?"

"I was going to break down at your house. I had to leave." Noah wanted to beg him to understand.

"You could've called me or texted or something."

"Yeah, I could have. I'm sorry." Why hadn't he?

Because you didn't want him to confirm he was leaving.

"Noah, I want this to work. I want something serious with you. Not just slipping over here or hanging out in the barn. I want something real. I want… God, I might as well just put it on the line. I want it all."

"All?"

Del shrugged. "You know. A future. A relationship that has the potential to… not end."

Noah's mouth dropped open. "You never even saw the same girl twice in high school."

"I didn't want to be seeing girls at all, remember?"

"Well, yes, but you…"

"Faked it well?"

Noah's cheeks got even redder. "Yeah."

"I haven't had any serious relationships since I ran from here, either. But that's because none of the guys I went out with were you."

"Del, I don't… I don't know what to say."

"There's nothing more for me to say either. If there's no way I can prove myself to you, then I don't know what to do. I've already offered to go out with you again."

"The first time didn't exactly go very well."

Del looked away, but not before Noah saw hurt in his eyes. "I had a good time, and I didn't run or get angry. You were the one who walked away."

Fuck. He had. Why was he so scared? "I think this is all moving too fast."

Del closed his eyes and took a slow breath. Noah knew he'd just hurt him even more. "It would feel too fast if I hadn't been wanting you every day for the last five years."

"Then why didn't you call me?"

"Maybe for the same reason you didn't bother to ask if I was leaving."

Noah studied him, trying to guess exactly what he meant.

"I was scared, so I just assumed you wouldn't want me. And I ignored what I wanted, what I needed."

"You needed to come home?"

Del nodded. "I needed to apologize and admit I love Crane Acres and want to be a part of it. I also needed to see if you'd forgive me."

None of those were things eighteen-year-old Del would have said. Noah doubted Past Del would've even thought them. "Yeah, if we'd actually been dating for five years, then this would be damn slow."

Del smiled then, and that made Noah feel a little less sick.

"Do you want me to back off and give you time?"

Noah didn't know what he needed, and that was a big part of the problem. "Maybe. Yeah."

"Okay. Whenever you're ready, call me."

"I don't know if…" If what? If he'd ever be ready? If he could ever trust Del? And yet the thought of not being with him hurt too damn much to contemplate.

"And if you decide it's never going to happen, call me to tell me that, so I know to stop hoping."

"Del, I… What about Clarice? I don't want her to think I don't want to see her."

"I'll have my mom bring her to the bakery. And your mom has offered to help when I need it."

"I'll help too. You know that, right? No matter what happens with us. I'll do anything to help with Clarice."

"Thanks."

Noah's eyes were drawn to Del's throat as Del swallowed and then looked away for a moment. "If you need someone to listen about things with your parents, I'm here for that too." Noah knew it was ridiculous to think Del would come to him as a confidant if Noah rejected him, but he had to make the offer.

He couldn't really walk away from Del, could he? But if

he didn't, he risked getting hurt as badly or worse than he'd been before.

Being hurt is better than feeling nothing. It's better than being afraid of success.

But this wasn't like his baking, was it? Goddammit, yes. It was exactly the same. He was afraid of disappointment, afraid of trying hard for something and not getting it.

"Things are better with Mom and Dad." Del's voice startled him out of his thoughts. "I talked to them yesterday. I must've gotten back to the house just after you left. I think I saw your truck speeding away, but there was so much dust that I couldn't tell it was you."

"I was driving way too fast. I was a mess."

"You were hurt. I get that."

"I wasn't fair to you. I shouldn't have just assumed."

Del shrugged. "I'm not sure I've earned fair treatment."

"Everyone deserves fair treatment. Unless they're like a serial killer or something."

Del smiled at that. "I guess it's good to know I rank higher than serial killers with you."

"You… God, Del. I care about you so much. I never stopped, but this isn't easy."

"I knew it wouldn't be. I should be happy, because things have actually gone so much better than I thought they would. But I still want more."

"I wish that I—"

Del shook his head. "One more thing before I go, okay?"

"Okay."

Del reached for him, cupping his face and drawing his thumb over Noah's cheekbones. Noah shivered, but he moved closer, letting Del know it was okay to keep touching him. He wanted whatever Del was willing to give him, because if he couldn't bring himself to stop being a coward, it might be the last time they touched.

Del gripped his hips, tugging him closer, then he brought his mouth down. At first, his lips were barely there, brushing over Noah's with exquisite gentleness. Then he traced Noah's mouth with the tip of his tongue.

Noah wrapped his arms around Del's neck and slid his fingers into Del's hair. "More," he whispered.

Del kissed him harder then, and Noah opened for him, letting him slide his tongue into Noah's mouth and sucking it until Del moaned. He wanted to pull Del toward the bedroom, but he didn't. Taking this further wouldn't be fair; his signals were mixed enough as it was.

When Del finally pulled back, they were both breathing raggedly. "I think I better go."

Noah reluctantly dropped his hands from Del's hair. "Okay."

"Call me," Del said, his voice so sad Noah almost reached for him again.

"I will. I promise."

Del walked toward the door, but Noah called out to him.

"Yes?" He didn't turn around.

"I'll be making unicorn cupcakes on Tuesday."

"I'll make sure Clarice is there."

"Okay. Um… Goodbye."

"Goodbye, Noah."

When the door closed behind him, Noah's house felt emptier than it had ever been. What was he doing letting Del walk away? He almost ran after him, but he couldn't talk to him again until he knew what he wanted.

He closed his eyes. How the hell was he going to figure that out?

EIGHTEEN

Noah actually managed to sleep in a bit the next day. After a breakfast that consisted of leftovers he'd brought home from work the day before, he started baking. By late afternoon, he had five pans of muffins, six loaves of bread, and three pies, each with a different type of crust. In desperation, he called Marty. If he didn't talk to someone, he was going to bake so much his kitchen wouldn't be able to hold it all.

Marty answered on the second ring. "Hey, Noah. What's up?"

"Um… I'm stress baking, and I think I need an intervention before I make enough to feed the whole town."

"Do you want me to come over?"

"Actually, I think I need someone to force me to leave the house."

"All right. Jolene's?"

"Um… how about Italian? In Sheridan."

"Uh-oh, is this a take-you-out-and-get-you-drunk kind of intervention?"

"Yes. Definitely."

"Should we ask Oliver to come with us?"

Noah considered that. Marty had a bit of a crush on Oliver when he first met him, but once he realized Oliver was completely in love with David, he'd been happy to just have a new friend. Noah didn't know Oliver well yet, but he liked him, and Oliver was more likely than David—who Noah often called Mr. Positive—to be honest about how bad it was having a boyfriend in Anticipation. "Sure. Oliver might not want anything to do with me after tonight, but—"

"I think he can handle it. I'll pick you up in a few hours, okay?"

"Perfect." That would give Noah time to deal with the rest of the dough he'd stirred up.

MARTY WAS LATER THAN NOAH EXPECTED, WHICH WAS FINE, because when he knocked, Noah was just pulling on his sweater after washing all the flour out of his hair. Stress baking tended to get messy.

When Marty and Oliver stepped inside, they both stared at the kitchen table.

"You really did go crazy, huh?" Oliver asked.

Marty gave Noah a once-over. "You went all out getting ready too. I feel underdressed."

He wasn't at all. He had on black skinny jeans and a lavender shirt, which was a fantastic color for him, and the sleeves were rolled up, displaying his tattoos. He was also wearing eyeliner, eye shadow, and possibly a light lipstick. Surely his lips weren't naturally that pink. "You look fantastic."

His cheeks were now far pinker than his lips. "Thanks."

"Do you two want some bread to take home? And maybe a pie?"

Oliver studied the bounty on the counter. "Um…"

"Please say yes."

"Yes!" Oliver practically jumped up and down.

Marty laughed. "Okay, yes."

Once Noah had packaged up baked goods for them, they headed out. On the drive, Noah insisted on talking about Oliver's latest writing project and ideas for new baked goods. He needed alcohol before he'd be ready to talk about Del.

Fortunately, their server approached them as soon as they were seated at DaVinci's. "What can I get you to drink?"

"I'll have this." Noah pointed to a vodka cocktail on their specialties list that sounded like it had enough alcohol to give him a buzz just by smelling it.

She grinned at him. "You got it. And for you, sir?"

"A glass of prosecco, please," Marty said. Oliver asked for the same.

"I'll be right back with those."

"So it's bad, huh?" Marty asked when she'd left.

"Yeah."

"Shit. What did he do?" Oliver asked.

"He didn't do anything. But I thought he did, and I…"

Marty winced. "Accused him of… something."

"Yeah. I really fucked up. But…" He shook his head. "No, I can't defend myself. I suck."

Oliver frowned. "And he's pissed at you?"

"He should be, and I guess he is, a little, but not like I thought he'd be."

"So…" Marty leaned forward, encouraging him to keep talking.

"I don't know what to do. I don't know if I can ever trust

him." He dropped his head into his hands. "God, why am I telling you all this?"

The waitress returned with their drinks, preventing Noah from spilling even more of his embarrassing story.

They ordered food—chicken parmesan for Noah, which he'd been craving since he'd smelled Ella's baking, pasta alla vodka for Marty, and mushroom risotto for Oliver. Then they were alone again.

"I'm not going to share anything you tell me. I promise," Marty said.

Oliver nodded. "Me either."

Noah took a sip of his drink and then another. "Thanks. I don't usually talk about stuff like this. I just… I don't know."

"Keep it all inside and brood?" Marty asked, toying with his wine glass.

"Hey!"

Marty shrugged. "You seem like the type."

"What does that mean?"

"Nothing bad, just that you're not one to open up easily."

"Neither are you. You hardly even talk at work."

Oliver's eyes widened, and Noah instantly felt bad. "Forget I said that. My problems are nothing compared to the shit Marty's dealt with. Del's a little flighty and arrogant, but basically he's a good man. He wants us to be together, and I don't even know why I'm fighting this."

"You don't have to justify being upset. I got out of my situation, and I've put my shit in the past. I just want to start over." Marty glanced at Oliver. "I had an ex who abused me. It took me a while to get my feet under me, but things are a lot better now."

"Shit. I'm sorry. I'm glad you got away."

Noah nodded. "Me too."

"Thanks. I have some news, actually. But I kind of feel

bad telling it since Noah and his mom have been so helpful to me."

"What?" Noah braced himself for more criticism.

"You know how you told me I should work toward opening my own catering business?"

"Yes, and I meant it." Had he applied to school? Was he leaving town?

"You know how David's friend Rob is living at his ranch now?"

Noah nodded.

"He wants to hire and a cook and housekeeper."

"Oh my God, did Rob hire you?" Oliver asked. "You know he and David have been friends for ages, right?"

Marty nodded. "He hasn't hired me yet, and I don't know that he will. But he came into the bakery yesterday and asked Lisa if she knew anyone who would be a good candidate. She asked me if I was interested right in front of him."

Of course she had. "At least I'm not the only one Mom puts on the spot."

Marty snorted. "It turned out all right. I doubt I would've sought out a position like that, but Lisa pointed out that I'd get a chance to try out a lot of new recipes, so I said yes. When Rob found out I make a lot of the food we've delivered to him, he set up an interview with me right then."

Marty's face was getting redder every second. Was that just because he had a hard time admitting how good he was in the kitchen? "And?"

"I went out to his ranch this morning to talk to him and do a cooking demo. He said he'd call me tomorrow."

"That's awesome," Oliver said. "Do you know if he's interviewed anyone else?"

"No, but I'm sure if he has, they were all less idiotic than me. I burned my myself." He held up his right hand, which had several band-aids wrapped around his fingers. "He caught me staring at him, and I hadn't even heard what he'd asked me. I was so nervous and…"

"What?" Noah asked.

"Well… I mean he's…"

"Hot as fuck?" Oliver suggested.

"Yes. Looking at him would be the easy part of the job."

Noah giggled, which probably meant he was drinking too fast. "I can guess what would be the *hardest* part."

"Oh my God." Marty flipped him off. Then he sighed. "He probably won't hire me though, not after I was such a hot mess."

"He probably knows you were nervous," Oliver said. "Noah and Lisa will vouch for you, and so will I."

"What if I do get the job, and then he decides I'm an idiot?"

When Noah shook his head, the room wavered. Yep, he was drinking too fast. "You won't be, and who knows, he might feel the same way you do."

Marty shook his head. "Even if he's gay"—he looked at Oliver as if wondering whether Oliver knew—"a man like that is not going to want a guy like me."

"An adorable twink with far too many tight shirts?" Noah asked.

Marty rolled his eyes. "He's what? Thirty? And all bearish."

Oliver held up his hands. "I think you're right about his age, and I've caught him looking at men before, but he hasn't said anything openly around me."

"There've been rumors he was at a gay club in Billings, but I can't be sure if they're true. You didn't get any clues when you were there?" Noah asked, not that he thought Rob had hung up Pride flags in the kitchen or anything.

Marty shook his head. "One time I thought he was checking me out, but he might've just been staring because I dropped a pan and the sound echoed really loudly."

Noah grinned. "Maybe, but none of us knew about David until Oliver came along."

Oliver's cheeks turned pink. "I didn't know either at first."

Marty took a sip of his drink, seeming to contemplate that.

"Will you take the job if he offers it?" Oliver asked.

"I guess so."

"Yes, you will," Noah declared.

"What about the bakery?"

"We'll find someone. It'll be summer soon, and we'll have more options. Don't worry about us. Do what's right for you," Noah said.

"Thanks. Now tell me more about you and Del."

Noah shook his head. "I'm getting buzzed and feeling good, and I don't want any more bullshit. Let's talk about this look you have going."

"Really?"

"Yes, it's awesome."

"You think so? I was kind of worried about wearing it, but Oliver told me to go for it, and I decided if you were embarrassed or something—"

"Hey. Don't ever worry about that. You be who you are, okay?"

Marty nodded. "Okay."

Noah ordered another drink, and they kept talking. They moved from makeup to shoes to movies and movie stars to what age they were when they realized they were gay; basically anything that wasn't Del. Noah also made sure their server kept the cocktails coming.

When they'd finished eating and paid their bill, Marty asked if Noah wanted to head home or go to Roar. It wouldn't be very crowded on a Monday night, but they could still dance.

"Dancing. I like dancing."

"Oh God, you're so drunk. I'm not even sure Roar will let you in, and God knows they aren't picky."

Noah wrapped one arm around him and the other around Oliver. "They'll let me in. They love me."

He swayed, and Oliver helped him right himself. "Is that where you usually…"

"Pick up guys? Yeah. It's been waaaay too long."

Marty shook his head. "I know things are a mess right now, but should you be…?"

"No hookups tonight. Just dancing."

"If you're sure…"

"Oliver hasn't had a chance to go out since he moved." Noah turned his way. "I bet you're a goooood dancer. You can dance with me, and Marty can find himself a man."

Marty shook his head. "I think Oliver and I should both stick with you."

Roar was only a few blocks away, but to Noah the walk took ages. When they were nearly to the door, he tripped over something, and Marty caught him. "Are you all right?"

"I love Del." He had no idea why he'd blurted that out, but once the words started, he couldn't stop himself. "I've been in love with him since I was fourteen. But he's an asshole. He left me."

Oliver frowned. "Maybe you should go home and sleep this off."

"No. I'll dream about him. It fucking sucks. Del does too, and he's—"

"TMI!"

Marty's horrified expression made Noah laugh, but once he got started, he couldn't stop.

Marty tugged on his arm, trying to make him stand up straight. "If we're going in, you've got to pull yourself together."

Noah took a few deep breaths. "Calm. I'm calm." Then he started laughing again. Finally, he wound down. "All good now."

"I hope you can stay that way. We'll dance for a little while, but I'm keeping an eye on you."

"Okay." He let Marty and Oliver tug him toward the door.

When they got into the club, Noah managed to walk a more or less straight line to the dance floor. Once he was in the midst of the crowd, the music consumed him. He moved with it, losing himself. A while later, Marty pushed in front of a guy who was trying to crowd up on Noah.

Eventually, a dark-haired man caught his attention. He could only see the back of him as he ground up on the man he was wrapped around. For a moment, Noah thought it was Del. Even after the man turned his way, and he realized it wasn't, he felt sick.

"Come on." Marty must have seen some warning sign. He steered Noah through the crowd, and Oliver followed close behind them. They made it into a bathroom stall before Noah expelled what felt like everything he'd eaten all week. Only a serious horror of what might be on the floor kept him from lying down right there.

Oliver held him up while Marty rushed to the sink, returning a moment later with a damp paper towel. "Wipe your mouth, and let's get you out of here."

"Can't you just let me die here?"

"Your mother would kill me, and I bet Del would help her. He might kill me anyway."

"No. He said he'd leave me alone." Were his words as slurred as he thought? "It's my choice."

Marty shook his head. "If he thinks we hooked up tonight, he's not going to be happy."

"He knows I wouldn't… That I… Oh shit." He turned back to the toilet. Apparently, he'd only thought there was nothing left inside him.

When he finished, he went to his knees, no longer caring how nasty the floor was. Marty got him more paper towels. After he'd cleaned off his face, he managed to stand, even though he was shaking like Mrs. Lyndon's Chihuahua.

"All right?" Oliver asked.

"No."

Marty sighed. "I'm going to get you some water and pay our tab. Then we're going home."

Water sounded so good. "Thank you. I'd kiss you, but my mouth is gross."

"Yeah. Don't do that."

Noah nodded and then regretted it. "How cheap was that vodka to give me a hangover already?"

"I think the quantity is more to blame than the vodka itself," Oliver said.

"I drank a lot?"

"You did."

He took Marty's hand and stumbled along behind him.

That was the last thing he remembered until Marty shook him awake later. "I've got to get you inside."

He blinked, trying to clear the fuzziness from his vision. "Inside?"

"Yeah, we're home."

"But we were…"

"At Roar. Then you passed out in the car. At least you let me get you to the car first."

"I'm sorry."

"It's okay. Someday I may need you to return the favor."

"Oliver?" He had been there, right?

"I already dropped him off." At least he hadn't hallucinated Oliver.

When they reached the door, Noah didn't think he could make it to the bed, so he just lay down on the couch, which he'd finally glued back together. "We broke the couch."

"What? When?" Marty frowned. "It looks fine to me."

"Me and Del. We broke it, but I fixed it."

"Wow, you really do have a fucked-up relationship with him."

"Yeah. I do." Noah let his eyes drift closed after that. "Bye, Marty."

NINETEEN

Del sat on the bench swing on his parents' back porch. It was late and everyone else was asleep. He had the monitor he still used for Clarice at his side, in case she needed him. For now all was quiet, and he was enjoying the stillness. Spring was well on its way now. He heard the hum of insects, and there was enough light from the house that he could see bright buds on a few of the early flowers.

All that promise of new life and new chances would mean nothing if Noah decided he could never trust Del. Whether they got back together had to be Noah's choice. If he said no, Del would accept it. He didn't have the right to push. But could he stay in Anticipation knowing there wasn't a chance for them? Had he been crazy to come back here in the first place?

No, it was good for Clarice. She'd had fewer nightmares since they'd settled in at the ranch, and he no longer noticed her pausing while playing and looking scared or pale. Most of the time, she was the sunny girl she'd been before she lost her mother. Some of that likely came from having attention lavished on her by so many people, and part of it came from having the horses to focus on. There was so much for her to do here when she wasn't at school, unlike in Chicago where she'd only had her nanny to play with.

But he also knew Clarice could thrive somewhere else, especially after having some time here. They could visit often, if he continued to do contract work. He hadn't told Noah this, but the company in LA had made it clear they'd have more work for him if they were satisfied with how he fulfilled the first contract. He could move out there if he wanted to, and there were plenty of other opportunities waiting for him.

He blew out a long breath. He didn't want any of those opportunities. He wanted Noah. And he wanted what was best for Clarice. For now, at least, that meant staying here.

He'd told Noah he'd give him time, but he was already about to combust from impatience. If he'd told Noah he still loved him earlier, would that have made a difference? He'd almost said it the last time he'd seen him, but he'd held back. Would hearing those words help Noah trust him?

He'd find out tomorrow after he dropped Clarice at preschool. It was time for him to lay all his cards on the table.

WHEN NOAH WOKE THE NEXT MORNING, HE THOUGHT someone was jackhammering just outside his window. Or maybe they were sawing, since it felt like he had sawdust in his mouth. Wait. That didn't actually make sense.

He tried to move, but his arm was all tingly, and his neck cricked from sleeping at an odd angle. Pain shot through his head when he rolled over. Maybe he'd broken his neck, and he was dead. No. It shouldn't hurt to be dead, should it? He hoped not.

He tried to move again, but nearly every inch of his body protested. His leg banged against something, and he realized he didn't have a pillow. After a few more minutes of pushing through the layers of fog in his head, he realized he was on the couch. Why?

When he attempted to sit up, his stomach told him in no uncertain terms that being vertical was a terrible idea. That jogged his memory. He'd been drunk. So drunk. He'd gone out with Marty and Oliver, because he'd been messed up over Del. He'd had a lot of vodka. A. Lot. The latter parts of the night were a bit fuzzy. He vaguely remembered being sick. Oh shit, he didn't throw up on either of them, did he? No, he remembered a bathroom and Marty taking care of him. He'd gotten him water and managed to drag Noah to his car. There'd been tears somewhere in there. Ugh. He had a feeling he owed Marty and Oliver an apology and a decent night out.

Once he sorted out what had happened to him, he realized he needed to pee desperately. As he walked to the bathroom —much slower than his bladder wanted him to—he noticed the sun was shockingly bright. What time was it? Shit, what day was it?

He relieved himself, took a few ibuprofen, and drank some tentative sips of water. Then he hobbled back to the couch. Apparently he'd danced a lot more than his body was used to. At least, he thought that was why he was so sore. A hangover didn't cause muscle pain, did it? He didn't think that was possible.

He picked up his phone and cringed at the brightness of the screen. Oh shit! It was nine AM on Tuesday. He was supposed to be at work at six. Why hadn't someone called?

Then he saw he had multiple texts. One was from Marty, saying he would take Noah's shift because he knew Noah wouldn't be in any condition to work. Another was from his mom telling him not to worry about coming in, then asking him to let her know he was okay once he was awake.

His fingers weren't working properly yet, so it took several tries to text her back. Finally he managed to say *I'm awake and fine. You sure you don't need me?*

A few moments later, she texted back. *Stay in bed. I'll check on you later.*

So he lay there—hungover as hell on a Tuesday when he was meant to be at work—and tried to piece together more of what had happened the night before. The only thing he remembered clearly was telling Marty and Oliver that he loved Del. He'd said it like it was obvious. And it was. It really was. He loved him, and he wanted to be with him. So why couldn't he just say that to Del?

He would. But he had to get himself together first.

Coffee. That would help. Maybe after a cup or two he could make more sense of things. The sound of the coffee grinder nearly killed him, but eventually the pot was burbling and coffee was beginning to fill the carafe.

While he waited, he drank some more water and stared out the front window. Was he really doing the right thing? He forced himself to imagine telling Del that he didn't want to be with him. Would it be easier not to make himself vulnerable, not to worry that Del would eventually leave? If he did say no, then he'd see Del all the time, see him and not touch him or kiss him. Ever. Again. Or Del would leave and then…

Hell no. He was going to Crane Acres, and he was going to tell Del how he felt and what he wanted—a life with Del and Clarice. He was going to offer Del his heart, because the truth was, Del already had it; he had for years.

But first he was going to make a cake. Apologies required cake, and he intended to apologize with the thickest, softest, most beautifully iced red velvet cake Del had ever had. Clarice wouldn't like the red, but this time, he was baking only for Del.

TWENTY

A few hours later, Noah was ready. He had a thermos full of coffee and the cake had been iced and placed in a metal cake safe he'd found at an antique store. He was going to drive to the ranch and ask Del to come with him to their favorite spot. With the snow melted, they'd be able to drive up there. They could sit and talk in the truck if they got too chilly.

He was looking in the mirror one final time and debating changing his shirt again when he heard a car in the driveway. Probably things had gotten slow at the bakery, and his mom was coming to check on him. He'd just tell her he was feeling better and had decided to run some errands since he had the day off. But when he looked out the window, he saw Del's truck.

He opened the door as Del came charging up the porch steps.

"I love you." The words seemed to burst out of Del. "I've loved you since our senior year. I was afraid of how I felt, and the longer I stayed away, the more afraid I got. Now that I'm afraid of losing you for good, could lose you, I can't hold back from saying it. I thought that maybe—"

Noah kissed him, cupping his face and holding him there while he tasted his lips, licking them, sucking on them, making Del gasp into his mouth. When he finally pulled back, he said, "I love you too."

"Y-You do?"

"Yes. I was coming to tell you. I made a cake, a red velvet one that Clarice will hate, but it's just for you. I have coffee too, and I'd planned for us to go to our spot. I was going to tell you everything about how I felt, but actually, I think 'I love you' kind of covers it all."

"So you want to try this? Us? A relationship?"

"I want to do more than try. I want to be with you, be your partner. I want everything. I know it's crazy and too fast, but—"

"Nothing between us is too fast."

"No?"

Del shook his head. "No."

"So do you want to go like I'd planned?"

Del grinned. "Yes!"

NOAH AND DEL DIDN'T TALK MUCH ON THEIR WAY TO THE ranch. The air in Noah's truck felt heavy with anticipation, and Del was worried that if he spoke he would break the spell and be back at the ranch.

As Noah put the truck in low gear and began to climb the trail to the ridgeline, Del laid his hand over Noah's on the gear shift and smiled at him.

"Is this real?" Noah whispered.

Knowing Noah felt the same uncertainty he did warmed

Del all over. “I hope so. I don’t want to have to work up the courage to do this all over again.”

“Me either.” Del pinched the back of Noah’s hand. Noah yelped and nearly ran them into the trees.

“What the hell?” “Sorry.” Their words ran over each other.

“I was just checking,” Del said. “But we’re still here. You didn’t dissolve into mist, and I didn’t wake up.”

Noah snorted. “I’d be the one waking up if you pinched me.”

“Fine. Get me back.”

Noah reached over and pinched Del’s thigh.

“Ow! You didn’t have to pinch that hard.”

Noah chuckled. “Seems like it’s real for both of us.”

“Good, because I have every intention of eating that cake.”

“Do you now? The whole cake?”

“I might let you have a piece, but it is an apology cake, right? So that makes it mine.”

“Asshole.”

They both laughed as Noah maneuvered the truck into a spot between two large trees.

After they parked, Del indulged himself by gazing at Noah with what was probably a very dopey look on his face.

“You want to get out of the truck or are you just going to sit there?” Noah asked.

“I’m contemplating what’s more comfortable. Here or the ground?”

Noah arched a brow. “For?”

“Eating you before I have my cake.”

Noah’s eyes widened for just a second, and Del loved knowing he’d affected him.

“I think I like that idea,” Noah said. “But it’s my turn.”

His turn? Del frowned. Did he really mean—

"It's my turn to be on my knees."

Del nearly choked. "Really? You…?"

"Yes. Go put your back against that tree." Noah pointed across the clearing.

Del still couldn't process this. "What?"

"You heard me."

"Wait. You still get to give the orders even though you're going to…"

"Blow you?"

"Yeah."

"Back against the tree. Now," Noah demanded.

That commanding tone was so hot. "But you—"

"Do you want me to change my mind?"

"No!" Del most definitely did not want that.

"Good. I'm going to set up our picnic, and then I'm going to suck your cock."

Noah took his time spreading out the picnic blanket and setting the cake and coffee on it as Del watched and waited, cock hard as steel, imagining how good Noah's mouth was going to feel.

Finally, Noah walked slowly toward him. He stood in front of Del for a moment just watching him, then he brushed his knuckles over Del's cheek, and Del drew in a shuddery breath.

"I love you," Noah said. "And you're more than worth the risk of a broken heart. I'd rather have you like this for as long as I can than be the one who runs this time."

"I…" Del opened and closed his mouth a few times, then swallowed hard. Noah's gaze seemed to follow his Adam's apple as it moved up and down. "I love you too. And I'm not going to hurt you. I don't want to be without you ever again."

Noah sank to his knees and Del stared down at him, still not really believing this was happening.

"Open your pants, and take your dick out," Noah demanded.

"So hot," Del whispered. He did as Noah said, even though his hands were shaking.

"Perfect." Noah leaned forward and licked the length of Del's shaft.

His tongue felt so good. And Del shuddered, barely able to keep still.

"Now—" Noah took Del's hands and put them on either side of his head. "Fuck my mouth."

"Noah." Del breathed the word out, too stunned for real speech.

Noah opened his mouth and looked up, trapping Del's gaze.

Del took a breath and then he pushed in, relishing the heat of Noah's mouth. "Feels so good."

Noah smiled around his cock, and Del pushed in deeper. Noah took it all, which only made Del more anxious to do exactly what Noah had said. He worked himself in and out as Noah's tongue slid along the underside of his cock. His strokes were tentative at first. Then Noah yanked on his hips and took him all the way down.

He thrust harder. When Noah showed no sign of discomfort, Del let himself go, driving into Noah's mouth as Noah moaned around him. He was close already. There was no way he could make this last. Noah was so gorgeous there on his knees, looking up at Del with love and lust in his eyes.

"Oh fuck, Noah. I… Fuck…" Noah swallowed as he came, taking every drop.

When Del finished, he pulled back. Noah wiped at his mouth, then stood and unfastened his jeans. "I want to come on your face," he said, voice rough from what Del had just done to him.

"Oh my God." Del's legs could barely hold him anyway, so he sank to the ground, hands shaking as he gripped Noah's hips.

Noah worked his cock and Del closed his eyes, ready for him. In seconds Noah's cum spattered his face. Then Noah was on his knees too, licking him clean and then kissing him so they tasted each other. They groaned as they clung together until, exhausted, they laid their heads on each other's shoulders and just held on. Del tried to remember how to breathe.

"Are we going to do things like this all the time now?" Del asked when he'd recovered a bit.

"As often as you can get away on your own. Or maybe you and Clarice can come for a sleepover, and I can get a really good lock for the bedroom."

"Or we—" Del froze, not sure how far he should go.

"We?" Noah looked hopeful. Had he guessed what Del was going to say? Did he want that too?

"Could move in together."

"Really? I thought you didn't want to leave the ranch."

He had said that, but at that point, he hadn't dreamed Noah would offer for him and Clarice to move in. "Living with you wouldn't be the same as me and Clarice getting a house. She could still see the horses most days, and I could go over there to help."

Noah frowned. "I thought you weren't working on the ranch, that you were only doing your consulting."

"I decided I like ranch work a lot more than I thought I did. I'm trying to work it out so I can work half time on the ranch and half on contracts."

Noah smiled. "I think that's great, and I know your dad must be thrilled."

"I haven't told him yet, but I'm sure he will be, and maybe we could eventually build on our own section of Crane Acres. Only if you wanted to." Noah didn't say anything, so he just rushed on. "There's plenty of space. We wouldn't have to be too close to my parents, but if you don't—"

"You mean that? You're really thinking about building on the ranch, about staying, about us making a life there?"

"Well… yeah."

"I love that idea. I want to be with you and Clarice more than anything, but we should ask her, shouldn't we?"

Del loved that Noah cared about how Clarice felt. "Yeah, we should."

"And we probably shouldn't rush things, no matter how much we want to. I wouldn't want your parents to think I'm trying to take you away from them."

"I'll talk to them about helping with the ranch first."

"Good, and we can make a plan about you and Clarice moving in with me. For now, we'll just see each other as much as we can."

Del didn't want to wait, no matter how right Noah was. "I want to be able to spend the whole night with you. Think of all the things we could do."

Noah raised a brow. "How much stamina do you think I have?"

"A lot more than I've seen yet."

Noah grinned. "That is certainly true."

Del was happier than he'd been in a long time, and he wanted to celebrate. "You owe me some cake now."

"Zip your pants and get over on the blanket."

"Are we eating cake or…?"

"I think we both need a rest."

Del sighed. "But you used that voice."

"I like how you react to it."

"Yeah, me too."

Noah cut them each a large slice of cake and put them on the paper plates he'd brought. When he held out a fork, Del snatched it out of his hand and scooped up a big bite.

"Mmm. That is amazing. Almost as good as sex."

"Keep making sounds like that, and we'll test that theory right here."

"Really?"

Noah rolled his eyes. "No. Eat."

Del did.

When they'd polished off two slices each and finished the coffee, they made out for a while. Neither of them seriously wanted to do more, but they couldn't resist touching each other. Eventually, it was time to pack up their things.

"When should we tell Clarice that we're officially boyfriends?"

Del smiled, loving that Noah was comfortable enough to use that word. "I was thinking we might do that this afternoon."

"Really? What about your parents? Are we telling them too?"

Del grabbed the edges of their picnic blanket. "I'll talk to them later, maybe tonight. I want to tell Clarice first."

"She might not be able to keep it a secret."

"It's not like they're really going to be surprised."

"True," Noah said as he tied up their trash in a plastic bag. "I think most of the town suspects already."

Del nodded. "And you know what?"

"What?"

"That doesn't bother me at all. I'm happy for them all to know that you're mine."

"Am I now?" Noah asked.

"Yes."

"Good. Because you're mine too."

Del barely resisted squealing with joy. "I thought maybe we could take Clarice ice skating. She missed the season where she could skate outdoors, but she keeps reminding me how I never took her skating in Chicago. There's still an indoor rink in Sheridan, isn't there?"

"Yes. That sounds perfect."

"Pizza afterwards?" Del asked, thinking this might be the best day of his entire life.

Noah frowned. "Does Clarice eat pizza? The sauce is red."

Del grinned. "She claims the cheese hides it, so it's okay."

"I should just accept this as three-year-old logic, right?"

"Yes, it's best not to question it."

"Then I'm in," Noah said as he took Del's hand and pulled him toward the truck.

TWENTY-ONE

Del held tightly to Clarice's hand as she shuffled forward on wobbly legs. They stayed close to the wall that circled the rink. She was moving especially slowly since her attention was riveted on Noah, who was showing off his tricks.

She giggled when he nearly fell over coming out of a one-legged spin. "He looks funny, Daddy."

"He does," Del agreed. "But I hope he doesn't hurt himself. We don't want to have to carry him out of here."

"No." Clarice shook her head. "I bet he's very heavy."

Del stifled a laugh as Noah skated back their way.

Clarice stretched out her hand, and Noah took it. When they'd made their way around again, Clarice said, "My feets are tired. They say they're done with ice skates."

"What would they say about walking down the street to get some pizza?" Del asked.

Clarice seemed to think very hard about her answer. "They say they would like to be carried down the street."

"What if the little girl they're attached to is growing like crazy and she's gotten too big for that?" Del asked.

"I am not too big," she insisted. "Noah can carry me."

Noah bowed low and skated a circle around them. "I am at your service, my lady."

She giggled. "See. He likes me."

Del rolled his eyes. "And you like getting your way."

"I do."

They made their way off the ice and changed back into their regular shoes. Of course Clarice insisted on putting her own shoes on with no help.

When she had finally determined which boot went on which foot, Noah scooped her up and gestured toward the door. "Lead on."

Del groaned. The two of them were going to drive him insane, but seeing them so happy was worth it.

The hostess led them to a booth. Del started to slide in beside Clarice, but she shook her head. "Uni sits there, because he's my friend. You sit there." She pointed to the spot next to Noah. "Because Noah is your friend."

After they ordered their pizza, Del reached under the table and took Noah's hand.

Noah mouthed "Now" and Del nodded.

"Clarice, sweetie," Del said.

She looked up from the coloring page she was working on. "Noah and I want to tell you something."

Her lip quivered, and her eyes got big. "Don't make me go back to Chicago. I want to stay here."

Del's heart ached for her. "Oh sweetie, we are going to stay here."

"That's right," Noah said. "I'd miss you too much if you left."

Del slipped out of the booth and moved to her side. "Come here," he said, helping her onto his lap.

"You know how you asked if we were boyfriends?" Noah asked.

"Yes."

Del relaxed when her expression changed from sad to hopeful. "We decided we wanted to be."

"You did?"

"Yes," Noah and Del said together.

Clarice squealed. "Is Noah going to live at the ranch now so he can be there all the time?"

"Not just yet. We were actually thinking we might live with him for a while."

She frowned. "What about the horses?"

"You could still see them almost every day."

"And I'd get to have Noah cook for me?" she asked.

Del looked at Noah and he nodded. "Yes, princess, you would."

"That would be the bestest!"

Noah slid out of his booth, knelt by Clarice, and took her hand. "Thank you for being so kind to me. I love your father, and I love you. I promise to do everything I can to make you happy here."

"I love you too!" She threw her arms around him, and several people in the restaurant clapped.

Noah's face turned bright red, and Del wanted to kiss him desperately, but he held back.

When Clarice finally let go of Noah, they all returned to where they'd originally been sitting.

Clarice went back to coloring as if accepting Noah into her family was no big deal. Some older kids got up and started playing one of the arcade games that lined the outside of the room where they'd been seated. The noises from the game and the kids' excited shouts drew Clarice's attention.

"Thank you," Del whispered. "For accepting her."

"Thank you for trusting me with her."

Del shook his head. "We're a bunch of saps now, aren't we?"

"Pretty much." Noah squeezed Del's hand. "I can't believe I thought I could ignore you once I got you home from the airport."

"Seriously? That was your plan."

"I thought that would be best for both of us."

Del wanted to be annoyed at that, but things had worked out so well. "Before I knew you'd be picking us up at the airport, I planned to stop by the bakery and apologize to you. I hoped that eventually you'd open up to the idea of being friends, but I was afraid I'd lost the right to anything more. Then I saw you and realized there was still something there. You didn't hate me after all, and just being friends would never be enough."

"I couldn't even pretend to hate you, especially after I met Clarice. She's amazing. And you're such a good dad. Once I saw you with her, saw how much you'd changed, I knew that I didn't simply not hate you, I still loved you."

Del put his arm around Noah and hugged him close. He didn't hold on for long; this wasn't a place for that. But that was okay, because he knew there would be plenty more hugs and hand holding in their future.

Noah lifted his beer and tapped it against Del's. "Here's to a future together."

Del clinked their bottles again. "And here's to our family."

"Oh, Del."

"You are my family. And this—you, me, Clarice—I want this to be forever."

"So do I."

"I'm going to see if my parents will watch Clarice tonight

so I can stay with you, because right now I desperately want you to kiss me until I can't breathe."

Noah's eyes lit up. "That sounds like a perfect idea."

They turned to watch Clarice then.

"She's so lucky to have you," Noah said.

"Not half as lucky as I am to have you both."

"You know how I said we should go slow on the moving-in thing?" Noah asked.

"Yeah."

"I was wrong. I'd help you move in tonight if that's what you wanted."

Del wanted exactly that, but he knew they had to wait at least a few days. "How about we talk to my parents tomorrow?"

"I like that idea."

Del reached under the table and took his hand. They laced their fingers together, and Del was sure he had never been happier—or more at home—in his life.

Dear Reader,

Thank you for downloading *Anticipating Rejection*. I hope you enjoyed it. Anticipation Book 1, *Anticipating Disaster* is available not and more *Anticipation* stories are coming soon. If you enjoy books with lots of heat, check out my *Love and Care* series, and if you're a fan of small town contemporaries, try my Ames Bridge series. I offer a free book to anyone who joins my mailing list. To learn more, go to silviaviolet.com/newsletter.

Please consider leaving a review where you purchased this ebook or on Goodreads. Reviews and word-of-mouth recommendations are vital to independent authors.

I love hearing from readers. You can chat with me on Facebook in Silvia's Salon, and you can email me at silviaviolet@gmail.com. To read excerpts from all of my titles, visit my website: silviaviolet.com/books.

Silvia Violet

ABOUT THE AUTHOR

Silvia Violet writes fun, sexy stories that will leave you smiling and satisfied. She has a thing for characters who are in need of comfort and enjoys helping them surrender to love even when they doubt it exists. Silvia's stories include sizzling contemporaries and paranormals. When she needs a break from listening to the voices in her head, she spends time baking, taking long walks, curling up with her favorite books, and hanging out with her family.

Website: silviaviolet.com
Facebook Page: facebook.com/SilviaVioletAuthor
Facebook Group: Silvia's Salon
Twitter: @Silvia_Violet
Instagram: @silvia.violet

ALSO BY SILVIA VIOLET

Lace-Covered Compromise

A Chance at Love

Coming Clean

If Wishes Were Horses

Revolutionary Temptation

Of Hope and Anguish

Three Under the Christmas Tree

Needing A Little Christmas

Anticipation

Anticipating Disaster

Anticipating Rejection

Anticipating (Coming soon)

Trillium Creek

Love at Lupine Bakery

Love at Long Last

Love Times Three

Love Someone Like Me

Love and Care

Father of the Groom

After the Weekend

Demanding Discipline

Painfully Attractive

Hungry (short story)

Pleasing My Valentine (short story)

Ames Bridge

Down on the Farm

The Past Comes Home

Tied to Home

Fitting In

Fitting In

Sorting Out

Burning Up

Going Deep

Getting Hitched

Thorne and Dash

Professional Distance

Personal Entanglement

Perfect Alignment

Well-Tailored (A Thorne and Dash Companion Story)

Law and Supernatural Order

Sex on the Hoof

Paws on Me

Dinner at Foxy's

Hoofing' It To The Altar

Wild R Farm

Finding Release

Arresting Love

Embracing Need

Taming Tristan

Willing Hands

Shifting Hearts

Wild R Christmas

25449783R00139

Printed in Great Britain
by Amazon